The Colwyn Bay Killings

Simon McCleave is a multi-million copy bestselling author. Before writing crime novels, he worked in television and film. He was a Script Editor at the BBC, a producer at Channel 4 and a Story Analyst in Los Angeles. He worked on films such as *The Full Monty* and television series such as the BBC Crime Drama *Between The Lines*. As a script writer he wrote on series such as *Silent Witness*, *Murder In Suburbia*, *Teachers*, *Attachments*, *The Bill*, *Eastenders* and many more.

AF173147

Also by Simon McCleave

DI Ruth Hunter

The DC Ruth Hunter Murder Case Series

Diary of a War Crime
The Razor Gang Murder
An Imitation of Darkness
This is London, SE15

The Anglesey Series – DI Laura Hart

The Dark Tide
In Too Deep
Blood on the Shore
The Drowning Isle
Dead in the Water

Psychological Thrillers

Last Night at Villa Lucia
Five Days in Provence

Simon McCleave

THE COLWYN BAY KILLINGS

canelo
CRIME

First published in the United Kingdom in 2023 by Stamford Publishing

This edition published in the United Kingdom in 2026 by

Canelo Crime, an imprint of
Canelo Digital Publishing Limited,
20 Vauxhall Bridge Road,
London SW1V 2SA
United Kingdom

A Penguin Random House Company
The authorised representative in the EEA is Dorling Kindersley Verlag GmbH.
Arnulfstr. 124, 80636 Munich, Germany

A CIP catalogue record for this book is available from the British Library.

ISBN 978 1 83598 191 7

Printed and bound in Great Britain by Clays Ltd, Elcograf S.p.A.

Look for more great books at
www.canelo.co | www.dk.com

To Neil, Sam, Mia, Macy and Tracey x

'No man has a good enough memory to be a successful liar.'

Abraham Lincoln

'To be born in Wales, not with a silver spoon in your mouth, but with music in your blood and with poetry in your soul, is a privilege indeed.'

Brian Harris

'Football is a staggering, heartbreaking, gorgeous, tommy-gun of soul-deadening, evil and beauty and I'm never sleeping again ever ever.'

Ryan Reynolds

PROLOGUE

It was a mild spring night as the young man tried to navigate his way through the log cabins of the Pen-y-Bryn Holiday Park. In his twenties, he was tanned, lithe and handsome, with a mop of curly black hair that framed his oval face. Finding it hard to concentrate or focus, he looked up to the clear sky where the moon sat between two bright stars. It felt like it was looking down at him. For a moment, there seemed to be a face on the moon's surface. One of the eyes winked at him. Shaking his head, the young man looked up again, but the face was gone. Was he seeing things?

Taking a step, he lost his footing for a moment but then regained his balance. He took a long, deep breath of fresh air in the hope that it would clear his head. Searching his memory, he knew that he'd been drinking for most of the evening but the dizziness just didn't feel like drunkenness.

Turning around, the young man surveyed the Pen-y-Bryn Holiday Park which was located on the North Wales coastline, just north of Colwyn Bay and a few miles south of Rhos-on-Sea. Colwyn Bay was a seaside resort that expanded in the Victorian era and overlooked the Irish Sea. Its famous pier was built in 1899 and included a 2500-seater pavilion.

The holiday park itself was relatively upmarket with a range of wooden cabins, as well as yurts and tee pees for those who wanted to go 'glamping'. It offered a variety of activities – archery, high ropes, pitch and putt, tennis – as well as bike hire.

I think it's this way, isn't it? Why can't I seem to remember?

Trying to get his bearings, the young man staggered along the footpath. In the distance, he heard the raucous laughter of a group of women sitting around a fire pit. He'd spent time with them earlier in the evening, but he wasn't going to go back. Not in his current state.

His head started spinning again. He really needed to lie down and sleep.

Then he got the eerie sense that someone was watching him from beyond the trees on the far side. Staring over, it was impossible to see if there was actually anyone standing there or if it was just his imagination creating the ghostly dark shadows as the branches moved in the silvery moonlight.

Looking down at the key fob in his hand, he saw that the key belonged to Cabin 5. Scanning his eyes left, he saw that he was now standing outside Cabin 7.

Nearly there, he thought, trying to focus his mind. He seemed to have no memory of the previous few hours. Had he really drunk that much? Or had someone spiked his drink? He was a man in his twenties so why would anyone spike his drink? *Was that even a thing?*

He took another step forwards. His legs felt like lead. It felt as if he needed to reach down and move the legs forwards with his hands. Then he laughed to himself at the strangeness of that thought.

Wow, I am seriously fucked. What's happening to me?

Dazzling lights shone from behind and he turned to see headlights. A car was speeding along and clearly not sticking to the 5 mph limit. Teetering off the road, the young man jumped out of the way as the car sped past, loud music and a thudding bass coming from its open windows.

Who the fuck was that?

Looking up, he saw the small wooden steps that led up to the door of Cabin 5. He held the thick handrail tightly as he took each step slowly, before trying to put the silver key into the lock. He could feel the rough grain of the wood beneath the palm of his hand.

It seemed to take an eternity for him to focus enough to slide the key into the lock but eventually the door opened.

I'm in. Thank God!

He slammed the door shut behind him, stumbled inside, shaking his head to see if he could clear it. Flicking on the light, he staggered into the living area that had a kitchen attached. The shape of the furniture and the kitchen cabinets seemed to blur around the edges. He had double vision.

Has someone given me Ket or something?

He took unsteady steps towards a long, inviting looking sofa and then let himself fall onto it. Nestling his face in a thick cushion, he sighed with relief.

Ah, that's so much better. I'll just stay here and sleep this off.

CHAPTER 1

What the hell is going on? Where am I?

Detective Inspector Ruth Hunter of the North Wales Police was struggling to work out where she was and why she couldn't open her eyes. Her eyelids felt like they had been glued shut.

Jesus! Why won't they open?

All she could hear were loud voices. She could sense people grabbing at her arms and chest and moving her.

What are they doing? This is horrible.

Then there was a crushing sensation on her chest. She couldn't breathe. It felt like an elephant was laying on her chest.

Bloody hell, this is agony! In fact, it's more painful than being shot.

Then she heard a man's voice. 'I'm going to need three milligrams of epinephrine please nurse. As quick as you can.' There was a sense of urgency in his voice.

A sharp pain in her forearm made her wince.

But then the panic started.

I can't get my breath! I'm suffocating.

She tried as hard as she could to drag the air into her lungs.

Nothing.

And then she started to get flashes of memory.

The events of the day began to play out in short bursts.

Earlier that afternoon, Ruth had been shot by DI Ben Stewart, a corrupt police officer from the Modern Slavery and Human Trafficking Unit, part of the National Crime Agency based in Manchester. It was the UK's primary law enforcement unit against organised crime and human, weapon and drug trafficking. Stewart had kidnapped DC Georgie Wild from Llancastell CID after she had discovered his criminal activities, but they had been stopped close to Menai Bridge. But not before Stewart had managed to shoot Ruth in the stomach.

Suddenly the severe pressure on her chest subsided. It wasn't that she could now breathe again. More that she just couldn't feel anything at all. A lovely floating sensation.

God, that feels so much better.

Then the male voice snapped, 'She's not responding.'

'Stats are dropping, she's gone into VF.'

'Charge the defib…'

'Stand clear… Deliver shock please. And resume CPR.'

The voices began to fade to a mumble before disappearing altogether.

In fact, that feels quite lovely, she thought.

In Ruth's mind's eye, she felt like she was floating up to the ceiling.

Down below she could see an emergency room in the Intensive Care Unit of a hospital. Doctors and nurses were desperately trying to resuscitate someone. As a nurse moved out of the way, she could see who was lying on the bed.

It was her.

The scene was in complete silence.

Jesus. I don't understand, she thought as she tried to make sense of what she could see below.

The heart monitor showed that there was no activity and that Ruth had flatlined. A doctor was performing rhythmic chest compressions as part of CPR.

A nurse rushed forwards with pads that were attached to a defibrillator and then placed them on her chest. Everyone moved back as an electronic shock tried to restart Ruth's heart.

Am I dead? Why do I feel so incredibly calm watching this? Ruth wondered.

On the other side of the emergency room, several figures watched on. A man in his sixties frowned and she realised it was her father who had died many years ago. Next to him, a woman in her thirties. It was Sian. Her partner who had been killed in a police operation three years earlier.

Then the whole tableau below her began to fizz with a white-gold light. The figures became blurred by its brilliance. Everything suddenly slowed as if in slow motion, and then it stopped.

Silence.

Ruth felt overwhelmed by a surge of great peace and serenity. Something was urging her towards the centre of the light, with the promise of such harmony and joy. For a moment she relaxed, as if allowing herself to be taken towards the light and all that if offered.

Wow. This is amazing. I want to stay feeling like this forever.

Then she caught herself as if she'd suddenly realised what she knew was about to happen.

No, no. I want to live. I'm not ready for this.

Everything went black.

CHAPTER 2

Waking slowly on the sofa inside, the young man looked around the holiday cabin where he had been sleeping for the past hour. It was still dark outside. His head was pounding and he had a splitting headache. He realised that he felt sick too. Then he vomited.

At first, he assumed it was a hangover. But then his nostrils stung with an acrid smell that made the air feel thick.

Smoke.

Sitting up, he felt his eyes water and sting. The whole cabin was filling with thick, bitter fumes.

'Jesus!' He coughed and gasped, trying to suck in air. It felt like he was drowning.

CRACK!

As he glanced over at the kitchen area, he saw it was engulfed in dark orange flames. The glass in the windows had shattered from the heat. Pieces of flaming fabric from the floor-to-ceiling curtains danced and bobbed in the air.

This is not good. I need to get out of here.

Trying to get to his feet, the young man felt his head swirl as though he was going to lose consciousness.

He stood up, trying to balance, squinting through the smoke. It couldn't be more than twenty feet from the sofa to the front door of the cabin, but it was impossible to see anything.

For a moment, he lost his footing and grabbed down at a coffee table to steady himself.

Why am I so bloody dizzy still? What's happening to me?

Putting one foot in front of the other, he moved towards where he had entered the cabin an hour earlier.

Don't black out, he growled to himself, knowing that if he did pass out, that would be it.

Suddenly his legs went from under him and he hit the floor hard.

It knocked the wind out of him.

Crawl! Just crawl.

Using his forearms, he attempted to move along the floor.

His lungs were burning with the hot smoke and the effort of trying to take in air.

Keep going!

His head was screaming at him to keep moving but his body just wasn't responding. His arms and legs were limp.

Digging his nails into the wooden floor, he tried desperately to move but it was as if he was paralysed.

It was no use. He was stuck there and he was going to die.

Putting his head down on the floor, he gazed over at an armchair that had now dissolved in flames.

He closed his eyes and waited for the smoke to overwhelm him.

CHAPTER 3

Looking out of the window of the Intensive Care Unit waiting area in the University Hospital in Llancastell, North Wales, Detective Sergeant Nick Evans could feel his stomach twist with anxiety. He ran his hand over his short dark beard and caught his reflection in the window. His hair was still cropped and made him look aggressive, but radically changing his appearance whilst he had been on the run had been vital.

Sitting nearby were Ruth's daughter, Ella and Ruth's partner, Sarah. They were both staring into space, lost in the terror of losing her.

Even though it had only been ten minutes since they had been ushered out of the emergency room as the 'crash team' arrived, it felt like hours. If the doctors hadn't managed to restart Ruth's heart in those ten minutes, then she would already have brain damage and it was unlikely that she would survive.

'This is unbearable,' Sarah muttered under her breath, sitting forwards with her hands clasped anxiously. Her dark chestnut hair cascaded onto her shoulders.

Ella looked at them both. 'This can't be happening,' she whispered as her eyes welled with tears. She looked so tired and drawn.

Nick could feel that his breathing was shallow and quick. 'What's taking so long?'

He didn't know what else to say. A trite 'I'm sure she's going to be okay' just wasn't appropriate.

They were left in an agonising silence as Ruth's life hung in the balance.

Nick was taken back to when he'd first met Ruth in the spring of 2017. When he'd learned that Llancastell CID were getting a new female detective inspector who was transferring up from the London Met, his reaction had been instantly hostile. He had assumed that she would be an arrogant cockney who would be condescending to the parochial yokel-local officers in North Wales. This wasn't helped by his active alcoholism at the time.

However, he found her to be the total opposite of this. Ruth had supported and encouraged him as he found his way into recovery. More importantly, they had become very close friends.

Suddenly the door opened, interrupting his train of thought.

Shit!

It startled him.

One of the male doctors – forties, glasses, wiry – who had been trying to save Ruth's life, came in and looked over at them.

Nick frantically tried to read the doctor's facial expression and body language. But he couldn't tell if they were about to get incredible or devastating news about Ruth. It was unbearable.

What is it? What's happened?

Sarah and Ella stood up in unison.

Nick held his breath. He felt sick and his pulse was racing.

'Ruth has suffered a cardiac arrest, but we've managed to get her heart beating again. And she is now breathing on her own,' the doctor said.

'Thank God,' Ella whispered as she reached for Sarah's hand.

Nick let out an audible sigh, shook his head and felt a tear in his eye.

'But we are by no means out of the woods yet,' he warned them. 'Her condition is extremely serious.'

'Will she be all right?' Nick asked anxiously. He didn't know what the doctor meant by that.

'The next few hours are going to be critical,' he explained gently. 'But Ruth is in the right place.'

Ella blinked nervously. 'Can she recover from this?'

'I think we just have to take this one step at a time,' he replied. 'The good news is that we've stopped the internal bleeding caused by the gunshot wound.'

Sarah shook her head and then asked, 'But she will survive, won't she?'

The doctor considered his response. Then he said, 'Ruth's heart stopped for several minutes. I'm going to arrange for her to have a CT brain scan to see if there's any neurological damage.'

There was a strained silence as they took in the news.

'Can we see her?' Nick enquired.

The doctor shook his head. 'Not for a while. I'd like to run these tests and then I'll let you know if you can see her after that.'

Nick nodded. 'Thank you,' he whispered.

CHAPTER 4

An hour later, Nick was back at Llancastell CID. Ella and Sarah had promised to call him as soon as there was any news and when they were able to see Ruth. He had been sitting in Ruth's office for ten minutes, trying to compose his thoughts. Taking a sip of strong hot coffee, he sat back on Ruth's chair and gazed at the tiny droplets of the Americano that had been trapped in the white plastic lid. The word *Hot Contents* had been stamped into the plastic.

His eyes glazed over as he stared at Ruth's desk for a few seconds. The photo of Sarah and Ella grinning and hugging in Ruth's garden. A smaller photograph of Daniel, the eleven-year-old boy that she and Sarah had temporarily adopted after Daniel's father had been killed. A plastic tray that contained a packet of nicotine gum. Ruth was trying to quit smoking yet again. Although he would never say it, Nick always thought that smoking was an integral part of Ruth's personality. It's just what she did. And her efforts to stop smoking seemed to jar against her distinct nature. Maybe that was just the addict in him. He remembered the first time she had uttered the words 'I'll smoke, you drive.' It had become their little catchphrase.

Looking over at her computer screen and files, Nick wondered if she would ever be able to return to work again. He tried to tell himself that the main thing was that she was alive. And if she had avoided brain damage and could live a decent life without being a copper then that was enough. Now that Ruth was in her early fifties, maybe she would take early retirement.

There was a knock at the door.

It was Detective Constable Jim Garrow. Tall, intelligent, with short brown hair. Garrow was known in CID as 'Prof'. It wasn't only because he had a degree from the prestigious Durham University. It was also because of his encyclopaedic knowledge and his meticulous attention to detail.

'We're ready for you, boss,' he said, gesturing to the CID office.

Nick looked out to where the detectives were assembled for the morning briefing. He had received a phone call from Superintendent Jones asking him to step in as senior investigating officer – SIO – and head of Llancastell CID.

'Thanks, Jim,' Nick said, trying to clear his head as he stood up and headed out into the office. He knew this was going to be difficult.

The atmosphere was understandably strained and tense. Usually there would be chatter and laughter but this morning the room was silent. The team were shocked and worried about Ruth.

'Morning everyone,' Nick said in a suitably serious tone as he looked out at the concerned faces of the CID team. 'As some of you know, the boss had a cardiac arrest last night. Her condition is now critical but thankfully stable. Her daughter Ella and partner Sarah are at the hospital with her. And they will contact me as soon as there is any more news.' He gave a half smile. 'All I know is that she's tough so it's going to take more than this to stop her.'

There were some murmurs of agreement in the room. Nick felt uncomfortable but he wasn't sure what else to say.

'And she would want us to continue to do our best work as police officers,' he added. 'Until her return, I will be acting SIO in CID. So, what have we got?'

There was a moment as everyone turned their thoughts from Ruth and got back into CID mode.

Garrow looked over and signalled that he had something. 'Lucy Morgan was arrested last night for the murder of her mother Lynne Morgan.'

Nick nodded. He knew it had been both an unusual and shocking investigation as Lucy Morgan had faked amnesia after slashing her mother's throat during an argument in a house in Wrexham.

Garrow looked down at his notes. 'She's appearing before a judge at Mold Crown Court this afternoon. I assume that she will then be on remand until trial.'

Nick raised an eyebrow. 'She's pleading not guilty?'

Garrow gave a frustrated nod. 'Yes, boss. Do you want me to liaise with the CPS?'

'That would be great, Jim,' Nick replied encouragingly. 'From what I know, this was quite a tricky investigation. Just make sure your notepad, interviews and forensics are all signed off.'

'Yes, boss.'

'What else have we got?' Nick asked.

Detective Sergeant Dan French looked over. 'Uniform have reported a fire over at Pen-y-Bryn Holiday Park in Colwyn Bay. One fatality.'

Nick frowned. 'Who called it in?'

'Local plod from Colwyn, boss,' French replied.

'Why are we involved?' Nick asked. If someone had died in a fire it wasn't automatically something that CID would concern themselves with.

'The chief fire officer thinks there might be something suspicious about it.'

'Okay,' Nick said. 'Why don't you and Jim go and have a look then.' Nick looked out at the team. 'Let's do our best work today everyone. I'll be in the DI's office if you need me.'

CHAPTER 5

Detective Constable Georgina Wild moved the pillows on her hospital bed and tried to sit up. Her ribs and left shoulder were still bruised from the car accident the day before.

The previous afternoon, she had been kidnapped by DI Ben Stewart, a corrupt police officer. Stewart had taken Georgie and his son Arlo hostage and gone on the run. There had been moments when Georgie was convinced that she was never going to survive. As she replayed the events of the past forty-eight hours, everything felt so surreal.

For a second, she remembered how Stewart had forced her to drive at gunpoint. As they had approached a police road block at the Menai Bridge, Georgie had swerved and crashed the car into a wall, while releasing Stewart's seat-belt. Georgie had been knocked unconscious and Stewart had been thrown through the car windscreen. It wasn't until she got to hospital that she heard the terrible news that Stewart had survived long enough to shoot Ruth.

Georgie felt a little twinge. Putting her hand onto her swollen stomach, she thanked whatever higher power was looking after her that her baby had survived the ordeal. She had been given various checks and tests when she arrived at the University Hospital in Llancastell the previous afternoon. The doctors in the pre-natal unit had reassured her that everything was fine.

For a moment, she thought about the baby's father, Jake Neville, who had been tragically killed only two months earlier. Jake had been an investigative journalist working on a story in North Wales when he'd been deliberately run off the road.

Georgie and Jake had gone out together during sixth form and had been inseparable. However, Jake had gone off to do a journalism degree at the London School of Printing after leaving school. Despite their promises to keep the relationship going, the inevitable breakup happened after about six months. They were too young and there were too many temptations for both of them.

And then, just over ten years later, they had bumped into each other by chance in Llancastell. After a few drinks, they had spent a wonderful night together at Georgie's house. When Jake left the following morning, she had wondered if they might have a future together. But he was killed on the way back to his hotel in Port-meirion.

With her eyes filling with tears, Georgie wiped her face and blew out her cheeks. It just didn't seem fair that Jake had been taken away at such a young age.

'You okay?' asked a friendly nurse who had come to check Georgie's blood pressure and pulse.

'Just a bit emotional,' Georgie admitted with a forced smile.

'Not surprising,' the nurse said, as she strapped the blood pressure machine to Georgie's right arm. 'I saw the news this morning. I don't know how you got out of that car in one piece.'

Georgie nodded. And now her thoughts turned to Ruth who was in the ICU in the same hospital. She couldn't help but feel guilty.

'I've asked about your friend in ICU,' the nurse said quietly. 'Ruth isn't it?'

'Yes,' Georgie replied with a nod.

'She's critical but stable,' the nurse explained, and then gave her a supportive smile. 'Don't worry. She's in good hands up there.'

Looking up, Georgie spotted two figures approaching. It was Pam and Bill Neville, Jake's parents. They had kept in touch ever since Jake's death. Georgie had told them about her pregnancy and her intention to keep her and Jake's baby. Pam and Bill couldn't have been more supportive.

'Hello,' Georgie said with a smile.

Bill was holding a beautiful bunch of flowers. 'We came as soon as we heard.'

Pam gave Georgie a kiss on the forehead and a gentle hug. Then she looked at her. 'Are you okay?'

Georgie nodded and then patted her stomach. 'Yes. I'm okay. We're both okay.'

Pam smiled as she sat down. 'That's all that matters then, isn't it?'

CHAPTER 6

French and Garrow weaved their way through the roads that dissected the Snowdonia landscape towards the north coast and Colwyn Bay. The sky above them was a growing mass of steel grey clouds that were slowly crawling across the sun like a dark, thick blanket. A few specks of rain splattered on the windscreen and the automatic wipers burst into life to wipe them away with an elegant sweep and then stopped.

Garrow was lost in thought. The past twenty-four hours had been challenging to say the least. He had developed feelings for Lucy Morgan while investigating her mother's murder and he had been completely taken in by her simulated amnesia. The discovery of her guilt had been so shocking. It left him feeling broken and idiotic for allowing himself to get involved with her.

'You watch that TV crime drama on ITV last night?' French asked. '*Unforgotten*. Really good.'

Garrow shook his head but was relieved to be distracted away from his guilt. 'The last time I watched a cop drama, I realised that I was watching what I do every day. Plus they got half of the stuff wrong which annoyed me.'

'Maybe I'm a bit weird, but I like crime dramas,' French admitted with a shrug. 'What have you been watching?'

'I'm on the last series of *Game of Thrones*. I'm a bit late to it but it's exciting stuff.'

French pulled a face. 'Oh God. Dragons, magic rings, ghosts. Not my thing at all. I don't like fantasy.'

'Actually, the narrative is based on the War of the Roses between the Yorks and Lancasters in the fifteenth century,' Garrow explained.

French gave him a withering look. 'And you wonder why we call call you "Prof" at work?'

Garrow shrugged. 'I'm not going to dumb myself down to fit in with you troglodites.'

'Troglodite?'

'It means "cave dweller",' Garrow replied with a smile.

'Jesus,' French said under his breath. 'I don't know why you can't use the word "twat" like everyone else.'

Garrow gave a wry smile as he looked out of the window. As they came over the brow of the hill, Colwyn Bay loomed into view. Beyond that, the Irish Sea swept away towards the horizon. It looked dark and sinister.

After a few minutes of silence, French looked over at him. 'I'm sorry about what happened with Lucy Morgan. Obviously I'm not sorry that we caught her but I know you got a bit involved there.'

Garrow shrugged. He couldn't tell French that he'd actually been in Lucy Morgan's flat when he'd realised her guilt and arrested her. 'You did warn me, Sarge. I've got no one to blame but myself.'

'Yeah, well I've avoided wearing my "I Told You So" T-shirt this morning.' French raised an eyebrow. 'Thank God you didn't do anything stupid like sleep with her. Then you would be truly fucked.'

And thank God he doesn't know just how close I did come to sleeping with her, Garrow thought, feeling incredibly uncomfortable.

The sign for the Pen-y-Bryn Holiday Park appeared and they turned left off the main road.

Within two hundred yards, they could see that the road through the park had been cordoned off with police tape. Two marked cars were pulled across the road to make sure no one had access. There were half a dozen or so uniformed police officers milling around in high vis jackets. Some of the holidaymakers were looking over and talking quietly.

'Here we go,' Garrow said, feeling relieved that he could change the topic of conversation.

As they pulled onto the grass verge and parked beside a smart-looking wooden cabin, they could see the burnt out shell of another cabin about fifty yards away. It was still smouldering. About twenty yards from the side of the cabin was the blackened shell of a car.

Two fire engines were parked alongside and fire officers were checking through the debris and pulling hoses back towards the vehicles.

'Who's our point of contact?' French asked.

Garrow glanced at his phone where he had the information listed. 'Jack Flaherty, the chief fire officer, and Sergeant Mel Robinson from Colwyn Bay nick was the first officer on the scene.'

As they got out of the car, the sun appeared from behind the clouds and a cool breeze blew in from the direction of the sea. The air was filled with the stench of smouldering wood as gulls cawed noisily above their heads.

Approaching a young male uniformed officer – twenties, dark beard, blue eyes – who was monitoring the police cordon, they both got out their warrant cards.

'DS French and DC Garrow, Llancastell CID,' French said. 'Sergeant Robinson about?'

'Yes, sir,' the officer said, and pointed to a uniformed officer in her late forties with short ginger hair and glasses. 'That's her over there.'

Robinson was in deep conversation with two fire officers.

French and Garrow approached, showing their warrant cards again. 'DS French and DC Garrow. We had a call to say that there's been a fatality and that the death might be suspicious?'

'Yes, that's right.' Robinson nodded and gestured to the older of the fire officers whose face was smeared with soot and dirt. 'This is our chief fire officer, Jack Flaherty.'

'From the position of the body, I would suggest that the victim was trying to get out of the cabin when they were overcome by smoke and died,' he explained.

'Any idea how the fire started?' French asked.

Flaherty pointed to the car. 'We think the fire might have originated in that car.'

French narrowed his eyes. 'Do you think it was deliberate?'

'That would be my suggestion,' he conceded. 'As far as we know, the car was parked and the engine was turned off. There was no collision. There seems to be no other explanation.'

'Do we know what time it started?' Garrow asked.

'The 999 call came in at 11:55 p.m.,' Robinson explained and then pointed. 'Guests in Cabin 6 were sitting out in their hot tub when they saw the flames. I've interviewed them and they didn't see anyone or anything suspicious.'

Garrow gave French a dark look. That meant that whoever started the fire in the car was now also responsible for the death of the victim in the cabin. So they had a major crime on their hands.

'Anyone else see anything?' French asked.

Robinson shook her head. 'Nothing so far. I've got my officers taking statements from everyone who was in the park last night.'

'Great.' French rubbed his face and then asked, 'Have you managed to identify the victim?'

'No,' Robinson said.

Flaherty gestured to the remains of the cabin. 'I'm afraid you're going to need dental records or DNA to identify whoever was in there.'

'Is there anything you can tell us that might help?' French asked.

'If I were to make an educated guess then I'd say the victim was young and male,' he replied.

French pressed the button on his Tetra radio. 'Three nine to Control, over.'

'Three nine, this is Control, receiving, go ahead, over.'

'We have a major incident at Pen-y-Bryn Holiday Park,' French explained. 'I'm going to need scene of crime officers on site as soon as possible. I'm also going to need two more uniformed units, over.'

'Three nine from Control, all received,' the voice on the radio said. 'Stand by and will advise, out.'

'Who's in charge here?' boomed a man's voice.

Garrow turned to see a middle-aged man, late fifties wearing a designer jacket, shirt, jeans and sunglasses, striding towards them.

French moved a few steps to intercept him. 'Can I help you, sir?'

'I'd like to talk to whoever is in charge here,' the man said irritably with a very middle-class accent.

'Can I have your name please, sir?' French asked calmly.

'Miles Hopkins,' he replied. 'This is my holiday park.'

French and Garrow both took out their warrant cards. 'DS French and DC Garrow, Llancastell CID.'

'I got up here just after the fire started but there was nothing we could do. Any idea what caused it?' Hopkins asked.

'Not yet,' Garrow replied. 'Is there anything you can tell us about the deceased?'

Hopkins' face fell. 'Deceased?'

French frowned. 'I'm afraid we have found a body inside the cabin.'

'What?' Hopkins spluttered. 'That's impossible. The cabin was empty. I've just checked the system and there was no one booked in there.'

French and Garrow exchanged a look.

'Well I'm afraid someone was definitely in there,' French said sombrely. 'And now they're dead.'

CHAPTER 7

Ruth felt that she had been in between wakefulness and dreaming for an eternity. It was exhausting. She continually dreamed that she had woken in her bed at her home in Bangor-on-Dee. For a few moments, she would feel such a sense of relief. She could even feel the warmth of the sunlight coming through the bedroom window and the smell of freshly brewed coffee. She fully expected to see Sarah walk in with a tray of toast and coffee any second. But then it began to dawn on her that this was actually part of the dream she was in. It kept repeating on a loop and felt like torture.

And then she fell back into the depths of the dream world that she seemed to be perpetually stuck in. The images, narratives, sounds and people in her head seemed to come in layers.

She was sitting in an old-fashioned room that smelled of old books and furniture polish. She had the feeling that she was very young. Maybe seven or eight years old. An evening sun lingered in the front of the home, painting the pale floral wallpaper of the large dining room with its tangerine sheen. The scents of grapes, cedar and sandalwood wafted in from the open door.

Ruth looked out of the vast window to her side. In the distance, just beyond the weedy gravel drive and the groomed descending lawn, as well as an erect spiraea hedge, lay a glimmering sea. It was so transparent it looked like silver paper merging with the bluish sky. A hint of nightfall was apparent in both the golden hue of the sun and the thinness of the sea.

Two women raced down the stairs and into the hallway. The click-clack of their old-fashioned boots echoed around the house. Ruth didn't know who the women were, but she felt afraid.

Then suddenly her Auntie Katie appeared, her hands gripping on to a striped dress as her face lit up with warmth, and a fuzzy halo of hair draped around her head. Ruth loved her slightly chaotic Auntie Kate who seemed to have such a big, loving personality that would fill any room.

Feeling her arm being pulled, Ruth was suddenly drawn back into what felt like the present.

Why is someone holding my hand? she wondered. It gave her a slight thrill as though this person who had taken her hand was a lover.

But then there were voices. And the noises of machines.

Come on, Ruth, wake up, wake up, she told herself.

But the idea of opening her eyes, of being conscious of wakening, just felt too draining and gruelling to contemplate.

And then something changed. There was a shift. Everything became soft, vague and gentle. She felt herself relax as though she was floating on a cloud. Why would she ever want to leave this peace and serenity. Why couldn't she just drift away into a blissful nothingness?

She was drawn away by the distant sound of church bells that were so redolent of Sundays and carefree summer days of childhood.

That's better, she thought to herself. *I'll just stay here for a bit.*

CHAPTER 8

Garrow and French were now in Hopkins' office in the main building on the site. There was a large oak desk at the far end with a padded office chair. The walls were adorned with framed rugby shirts and photos of a small private plane that Garrow assumed belonged to Hopkins. He got the feeling that he was both a know-it-all and a show off.

'Please, sit down,' Hopkins said, gesturing to a leather sofa and armchairs with a low coffee table to one side. His manner seemed to have softened in the past few minutes.

'Thank you,' French said, looking up at the framed rugby shirts.

From their white colour and red rose, even Garrow knew that they were English.

Hopkins looked lost in thought as his eyes roamed nervously around the room. 'Sorry,' he said blinking. 'This has all been such a shock. Can I get you some coffee or tea?'

French gave him a half smile. 'We're fine, thank you.'

Hopkins blew out his cheeks, shook his head slowly and sat back in his chair. He was clearly trying to take in the news about the fatality.

'Do you have any staff living on site?' Garrow asked, as he tried to get comfortable on the sofa. That was the thing with Chesterfield-style sofas, he thought. They looked nice but they were bloody uncomfortable.

Hopkins nodded. 'Most of the staff live here on site.'

'But not in the cabin that was burned down?' French asked to clarify.

'No,' Hopkins replied. 'The cabins are high-end, luxury. Staff on site normally live in the static caravans on the far side of the park... Not that there's anything wrong with them of course.'

Garrow pushed a strand of hair from his face. 'Do staff have access to those luxury cabins?'

'Not all staff. Obviously the keys are available when someone's been in there and it needs cleaning. That kind of thing. But it was empty last night,' he said, looking confused. Before he could explain more, his mobile phone rang.

Garrow and French exchanged a look as he spoke quietly on the phone.

He ended the call and then gestured to his phone. 'That was our site manager. Kevin, who runs our bike hire, hasn't shown up for work this morning.'

'Does Kevin live on site?' French enquired.

'Yes, he has a static caravan.'

Garrow, who had now taken out his notepad and pen, looked over. 'Can I have his surname?'

'Kevin Ball,' Hopkins said, now deep in thought.

'Any reason why Kevin would have been in that cabin last night?' French asked.

'No. None whatsoever. In fact, had he spent the night in a vacant cabin without informing someone, he would have been sacked.'

'Can we get someone to go down to Kevin's caravan now and check if he's there?' Garrow suggested.

Hopkins nodded. 'My site manager is doing that as we speak.'

A glamorous blonde woman in her late forties came in. She was wearing a fashionable scarf, designer coat and heels. She gave Garrow and French a confused look.

'These are detectives,' Hopkins explained. 'This is my wife, Jane.'

'I heard about the fire,' Jane said in a concerned tone. 'Was anybody hurt?'

French looked over at her. 'I'm afraid there has been a fatality, yes.'

'Oh God, that's awful.' She looked shocked. 'Who was in there?'

'That's the thing.' Hopkins pulled a face. 'It was empty. No one was booked in until tonight.'

'I don't understand.' The blood drained from Jane's face. She shot her husband a terrified look. 'I've been trying to ring Matty all morning but he's not answering his phone.'

Hopkins looked instantly uneasy.

'Matty?' French asked.

'Our son,' Jane said, as she pulled out her phone and tried the number again.

'He works here,' Hopkins said. 'He runs the shop and the cafe.'

'Does he live on site?'

Hopkins nodded. 'Yes. In one of our statics.'

Jane looked at Hopkins, pointed to the phone and shook her head. 'He's not answering,' she said, starting to sound frantic.

French sat forwards. 'Does Matty have access to the cabin?'

'He can get in,' Hopkins said, getting up from his desk with a sense of urgency.

'Oh God, what if it's him?' Jane looked at them and then gave Hopkins an accusatory glare. 'He kept complaining about the damp in that caravan. What if he just decided to use that cabin for the night?'

'I'm sure Matty is just sleeping off another hangover,' Hopkins said, trying to reassure her as they both headed for the door. 'But I am going to give him a piece of my mind for not answering his bloody phone.'

CHAPTER 9

Sarah sat beside Ruth's bed gazing at her chest as it slowly moved up and down. She reached over, took her hand and smoothed her thumb slowly over the back of it. Ella had gone to get coffees and any food she could find.

'I've spoken to Chris,' Sarah said, referring to Ruth's younger brother. 'He's going to drive down later today. And my mum sends her love, but she can't come in because of her chemotherapy. I've also explained to Daniel that you're not well but I've left it at that for the time being. He wants to see you but I'm going to hold off for a bit to see how you are in a couple of days.'

Sarah took a few seconds, let Ruth's hand go, and sat back in her seat. She took out her phone. 'I've been looking through all the photographs on my phone. And I found those photos we came across in that box from when you were a kid. There's that one your mum took of you and Chris in front of the telly during the Queen's Silver Jubilee. And you both look bloody miserable as sin. You did tell me why but I can't remember now.' Sarah's mouth formed a little smile. 'And we also established that I wasn't even born in 1977.' Sarah continued to look through the photos. 'And this one with your friends. You've got black ribbon tied into your hair Madonna style. You're standing with your friends all dressed up to go to a concert when you were a teenager. I can't remember if you said if it was

Duran Duran or Wham. I think it was Wham. And then there's those photos of us at Glastonbury the first time we met, and I was off my face on a pill. In fact, I can't even remember what band was playing. I think it was some dance act. I think it was Basement Jaxx. And some photos of Ella on the swings at Clapham Common.' Sarah felt her eyes well with tears and she took a deep breath to make sure she didn't just break down and sob. 'And I found the first photo we had taken together after you brought me back from Paris.' Sarah looked over at Ruth and smiled. 'We've been through a lot, haven't we? When you look back on it.'

The door opened and Ella came in. She was holding two coffees and a brown paper bag that had food inside.

'Hey,' Ella said with a kind smile. 'They didn't have prawn so I got you tuna and sweetcorn.'

'Great,' Sarah said gratefully as Ella came over and handed her the coffee, sandwich and crisps. 'Every time I have sweetcorn I remember how much I like it. But then I forget again, if you know what I mean.'

'Yeah,' Ella said. 'I know exactly what you mean.'

Sarah held up her phone. 'I've been looking at some old photos on my phone. Look at this one. It's you on the swings at Clapham Common with your mum. You can only be about two.'

Ella leaned, peered at the photo and rolled her eyes. 'It looks like she got me dressed in the dark. Nothing matches. Thanks Mum.' Ella shook her head. 'I can't remember that photo.'

'I'm guessing it was your dad who took it?' Sarah suggested.

Ella snorted as she went back to the other side of the bed and sat down. 'I doubt it. Mum told me he was never around when I was young and then he fucked off to Australia.'

'Yeah,' Sarah said with a nod as she sipped the hot coffee. 'But you saw him quite recently?'

'About two years ago. He was over and he made contact,' Ella explained. 'But I've only spoken to him on the phone a couple of times since then.'

The door opened and a young doctor with glasses came in.

Sarah was getting used to him and the nurses coming in and out to check on Ruth.

Having checked on her ECG, the young doctor looked at them. 'I've had a look at Ruth's CAT scan and her MRI. I don't want you to worry but I've seen some inflammation of the brain. Because Ruth had a cardiac arrest, it has triggered something called a cerebral edema. It means that her brain has swelled and the blood vessels have constricted.'

Sarah felt her stomach tighten with anxiety. 'Is there anything you can do?'

The doctor nodded. 'I think the best thing is for us to put Ruth into an induced coma. It is quite common in a case like this so there's no need to worry unduly. We will give her a mixture of anaesthetics.'

Ella frowned. 'Why do you need to put her in a coma?'

'It allows the body and brain to heal faster,' he explained. 'There is less pressure on the heart itself and the swelling on the brain should ease.'

'How long will she be in this induced coma?' Sarah asked.

'It's hard to say. We'll continue to monitor Ruth with CT and MRI scans. Sometimes it's a matter of days. But sometimes it can be weeks. And on the rare occasion, it can be months.' The doctor looked at them. 'I'm sorry not to have better news.'

As he headed for the door, Sarah shared a concerned look with Ella.

CHAPTER 10

Garrow and French had followed Miles and Jane Hopkins as they made their way over to the far side of the holiday park where the static caravans were lined in rows. As Garrow looked up, he noticed that the weather had changed quite suddenly. Bright spring sunshine had given way to dark, granite-coloured clouds. The atmosphere had become heavy with the smell of wet earth, which added to the air of dark anticipation. It felt like the darkness was swallowing the sky as the wind began to whip around them. A couple of people had come out of their caravans to take down their washing before the inevitable rain started.

A middle-aged woman looked over at them as she pulled a shirt from the line. 'Mr Hopkins? I heard about the fire last night. Everything all right?'

Hopkins, lost in his own thoughts and worry, didn't respond as they marched quickly across the field, aware that the heavens were about to open.

He and his wife had said virtually nothing on the way. Their anxiety was through the roof for obvious reasons.

Reaching a small cream-coloured static caravan, Hopkins went up the small staircase to the door and banged on it frantically.

'Matty? Matty?' he bellowed anxiously.

Meanwhile, Garrow and French moved around the caravan to see if they could see inside.

'Matthew? Open this door!' Jane cried.

Garrow cupped his hands as he peered inside. As far as he could see, the caravan was empty.

Trying the door, Hopkins found that it was locked. He looked at his wife. 'The bloody door's locked!'

'Well knock it down,' she snapped.

He took a step back, then hit the door hard with his shoulder.

Nothing.

He tried again and this time the door flew open with a crash.

Hopkins and Jane rushed inside.

Garrow and French followed them.

The inside of the caravan was cramped but neat and tidy.

Jane hurtled to the back of the caravan and threw open the bedroom door. 'Matthew?'

'What is it?' Hopkins asked.

'His bed hasn't been slept in,' Jane exclaimed. Her breathing was now shallow and full of panic. 'I don't understand.'

'Is there anywhere else he could be?' Garrow asked.

Hopkins looked concerned. 'Matty's a young man in his twenties. He doesn't always sleep here.'

'I know it's him up in that cabin.' Jane's eyes were full of tears. 'It's all our fault.'

'Come on. We don't know anything yet.' Hopkins put a comforting hand on her shoulder but she flinched it away angrily.

French's Tetra radio crackled. 'Three nine from Alpha four, are you receiving me, over.'

French headed for the door and went outside where he was joined by Garrow.

'Three nine receiving, go ahead, over.'

'Sir, we've found something in the burned out car that we need you to come and look at, over.'

It was one of the uniformed officers over at the other part of the site where the luxury cabins were located.

'Okay,' French replied. 'We're on our way Alpha four, out.'

Hopkins and Jane came out of Matty's caravan. Jane was trying to ring her son's mobile again.

A tall man in a baseball cap approached. 'Mr Hopkins?'

Garrow noticed that he had a name tag on his thin, dark green Pen-y-Bryn Holiday Park waterproof jacket – *Dylan Williams – Manager.* His cap also had *Pen-y-Bryn Holiday Park* on it in green lettering.

'Have you checked Kevin's caravan?' Hopkins asked.

Williams nodded. 'No sign of him, I'm afraid. I spoke to his girlfriend and she said that the last time she heard from him was about nine o'clock last night.'

Garrow looked at French. They had a young male victim and two missing people who fitted that profile.

CHAPTER 11

7 June, 1977

The London Borough of Battersea was decked out in red, white and blue. Bunting made of little Union Jack flags hung from every lamppost. Ruth, who was eight years old, made her way past the communal area of the Winstanley Estate. The concrete was cracked and strewn with weeds. An old Ford Cortina with no tyres had been left on bricks.

Two long trestle tables had been placed together and were now covered with paper plates and cups. Women from the estate were decorating the table with Jubilee ribbons and balloons. A large cardboard sign had *WINSTANLEY JUBILEE PARTY* written in black marker on it. Two women approached with trays bearing jugs of orange squash, red jellies and a homemade Jubilee cake.

'You coming down later, Ruthie?' asked a voice with a strong cockney accent.

Ruth turned to see Dolly Edwards – forties, blonde quaffed hair and an orange patterned blouse with enormous collars – giving her a kind smile. Ruth looked at Dolly's tight bell-bottom jeans. She wanted a pair just like them but her dad said they couldn't afford it.

Ruth was in awe of Dolly Edwards whom she thought looked like Farah Fawcett from the *Charlie's Angels* television show. She was so glamorous and the opposite of her own mum. In fact, she sometimes wished Dolly Edwards was her mum.

'I think so,' Ruth replied nervously.

'Come on,' Dolly said encouragingly. 'All the kids are coming down. You got a hat?'

Ruth frowned and then lied. 'Yeah.' She knew that lots of children on the estate had been making crowns or hats with Union Jack patterns. She had asked her mum a few times to help her make one, but her mum's response had been to get angry and tell her she would do it *later.*

Dolly smiled at her again. 'You've got a brother, haven't you?'

Ruth nodded but still felt embarrassed. 'Christopher.'

'Make sure you bring him an' all, okay?' Dolly said.

'Yeah.' Ruth nodded and scampered away. In her hand she had two magazines. The Silver Jubilee edition of *The Radio Times* and the newest edition of *Jackie* magazine. *The Radio Times* had cost 12p, *Jackie* 7p, and she'd bought a couple of cherry-flavoured bootlaces with the 1p that was left over.

Climbing the concrete stairs to reach her family's flat, she got the usual stench of urine, empty beer cans and rotting rubbish. Holding her breath, she ran up the stairs then headed down the long walkway to flat 73 where she lived with her mum, dad and younger brother, Chris. Some residents had decorated their windows with Union Jacks and bunting to celebrate the Jubilee. For some reason, they didn't have any bunting or decorations in their flat. She didn't know why.

Silver Lady by David Soul came blaring from some-where. Ruth mouthed to the lyrics of the chorus. Her mum said that David Soul was *a bit of a hunk*, but she wasn't quite sure what that meant.

Glancing over the balcony, she looked down at the communal area below where the preparations for the Jubilee party continued. She felt excited about the prospect of spending the afternoon stuffing her face with cake and jelly. And she got a little fizz of excitement at the prospect of seeing Dolly Edwards again.

Opening the door, she went down the hallway and spotted that her mum was ironing in front of the television. *Swap Shop* with Noel Edmunds was on.

'Dolly asked if me and Chris were going to the party this afternoon,' Ruth said.

'Oh did she?' her mum muttered. Ruth got the feeling that her mum didn't like Dolly. She'd heard her tell her dad that Dolly was a *stuck up cow*.

'Mum, me and Chris need a hat for the party.'

Her mum took the cigarette from her mouth as she turned over a pair of black trousers and continued to iron them. 'I haven't got time to sort out a hat for you. Can't you do it?'

'All the other kids are gonna have hats,' Ruth said with a frown.

'Yeah, well there's nothing I can do about that,' her mum huffed. 'Your dad's havin' a bath. Then me and him are off down The Wellington. You'll have to take Chris with you if you're going to that street party.'

'I thought you were coming with us?' Ruth asked, feeling disappointed.

'Stop pestering me, will you?' her mum said, sounding flustered.

Ruth slumped onto the sofa with a long face and looked at her *Jackie* magazine. There was a young woman on the front wearing a Jubilee T-shirt and holding a Jubilee mug with *Would Jubileeve It?* as the heading.

Looking up, she saw her dad walk in with a towel wrapped around his waist. His hair was wet and black. He smelled of Shield soap. She loved the look of the bar of Shield soap that sat on the side of the bath. It was a turquoise colour with other shades of light blue running through it. And it smelled really clean.

'All right, princess?' he said, ruffling her hair. 'Got my strides, love?'

Her mum handed him his freshly ironed trousers. 'I found a couple of quid in the back pocket.'

'Bloody hell,' he said with a grin. 'First round's on me then?'

Ruth began to thumb through the magazine. She could hear Chris playing noisily with Lego in the bedroom they shared.

Looking up, she saw that the band Showaddywaddy were on the television performing their latest single, *When*. They were all dressed in bright red Teddy Boy suits and black 'Brothel Creeper' shoes.

Her mum smiled and went over to the television to turn up the volume. 'Gotta love a bit of Showaddywaddy,' she said brightly.

Ruth continued to sulk. Her mum had promised to take her and Chris to the Jubilee street party.

'Cheer up, sunshine,' her mum said as she jigged around to the song. 'It might never 'appen.'

Suddenly, there was a loud banging on the door.

'Get that will you, love?' her dad shouted from the bedroom.

Her mum frowned and looked anxious.

There had been various incidents at their flat over the years. Men had knocked on the door looking for her dad because he owed them money. A couple of times her dad had been punched. Other times men arrived and had handed her dad stuff that they said was *a knock off*. And once in a while it was the police at their door. Her dad seemed to hate the police. He called them *The Filth*.

Ruth got up from the sofa and followed her out, along the hallway.

Her mum opened the door cautiously.

There were two uniformed police officers standing on the doorstep.

'Is Stan Hunter in?' the younger policeman asked.

Ruth spotted her dad move to the bedroom door to see what was going on.

'What's it about?' her mum asked in a hostile tone as she pushed the door so that there was only a small gap between them.

'Is he in or not?' the older policeman asked with a huff.

Her dad made a sudden move towards the front door and pulled her mum out of the way.

'What the fuck's going on?' he demanded angrily.

'I'm gonna need you to come down the station with us,' the younger officer explained.

'What the hell for?'

'Come on, Stan,' the older policeman said in a tone that suggested he knew her dad. 'Just a few questions.'

'Piss off,' her dad growled. 'It's Jubilee Day for fuck's sake. I'm spending time with my family.'

Ruth was confused because her dad and mum were going to the pub and leaving her and Chris on their own.

The younger officer put his hand on her dad's shoulder.

'Don't fucking touch me!' her dad thundered.

A scuffle broke out and punches were thrown.

The fight moved out to the walkway.

The police officers wrestled her dad to the ground, pulled his hands behind his back and put handcuffs on them.

'Jesus, Stan,' the older policeman sighed. 'It didn't have to be like this, did it?'

Ruth felt sick with anxiety as the officers pulled her dad to his feet and began to march him down the walkway. Several neighbours had come out to see what all the commotion was about.

Taking a few steps outside, Ruth watched her dad go. Then she peered over the balcony. She saw Dolly looking up at her with a concerned expression.

Ruth's mum came to her side and looked down to see what Ruth was looking at.

Ruth saw Dolly and her mum lock eyes for a second.

'Come on, Ruth,' her mum snapped, clearly embarrassed. 'Get inside will you?'

'Can we still go down to the party, Mum?' Ruth asked as her mum ushered her into their flat.

'No,' her mum said angrily. 'I'm not going down there with all that lot judging me. You'll have to watch it on the telly.'

Her mum turned and slammed the front door shut and then locked it.

CHAPTER 12

Garrow and French had made their way back across the Pen-y-Bryn Holiday Park site. The park was slowly coming to life with holidaymakers setting off on walks, cycling and heading for the coast. A middle-aged couple came jogging past with their golden retriever running by their side.

As they arrived back at the scene of the fire, Garrow noticed that the scene of crime forensics van had arrived. There were various SOCOs, dressed in full white nitrile suits, masks and rubber boots, starting to sift through the burnt debris of the cabin – which was now a major crime scene. The fire service would also provide their own specialised fire investigation officer who would work in tandem with the forensics unit.

Sergeant Robinson approached. She was holding a large transparent plastic evidence bag.

'You found something in the wreckage of the car?' French enquired.

Robinson nodded with a serious expression as she held up the bag. Inside was a blackened shotgun.

French cast a knowing glance at Garrow. It was definitely a significant find.

'Can I have a look?' Garrow asked as he reached out to take the bag. Scanning the gun for markings, he soon saw the indentations on the gun's long steel barrel – *James Purdey & Sons*.

'What do you think?' French asked.

'Purdey shotgun. Probably the most popular shotgun in the UK,' Garrow said. 'They are also the Royal Family's shotgun maker of choice.'

French gave Robinson a dry smile. 'Sometimes it's useful working with a walking encyclopaedia.'

'I can see that,' she said with a grin. 'I'll hand it to the forensics team.'

Garrow was used to French's little digs and knew that he didn't mean anything by it.

French gestured to Garrow that they should return to the burned remains of the cabin where the SOCOs were now busy working.

'Do we think the shotgun is linked to the fire?' Garrow said, thinking out loud as they walked across the grass that was strewn with black fragments of wood from the fire.

'Maybe. Although you know what it's like in North Wales. The world and his wife seem to have shotguns,' French said as he looked over at the blackened shell of the car. 'Doesn't look like we're going to get anything from the number plates.'

Garrow nodded. The number plates were nowhere to be seen and must have been destroyed in the fire.

'Hopefully we can get the VIN number off the chassis and trace the owner that way,' Garrow suggested. The car's VIN – vehicle identification number – was the identifying code for the specific vehicle. Essentially it served as the car's fingerprint.

As they approached the crime scene, a young female SOCO handed them forensic suits, masks and boots.

Pulling on the suit, Garrow got the familiar chemical smell from the nitrile material. He slipped on the white rubber boots and then followed French. The forensic team had now placed aluminium stepping plates down across the charred remains of the cabin to preserve the crime scene and any forensic evidence.

Three SOCOs were crouched down over a black shape. One of them was taking photographs, while another used tweezers to remove tiny fragments of evidence. The air was thick with the acrid smell of burned wood.

Garrow tried not to look too hard at the body. Even though he had now seen his fair share of dead bodies, the grisly sight of a corpse that had been severely damaged in a fire wasn't something he would ever get used to.

'There they are,' boomed a familiar voice.

They turned to see Professor Tony Amis, dressed in a full forensic suit, approaching. Pulling down his mask, he gave them a smile. When Garrow had first met him, he had thought that Amis' jolly nature was ill-judged and even inappropriate. But he now realised that his coping mechanism was to detach himself from the hideous crime scenes and dead bodies that he spent so much of his working life around.

'Hi Tony,' French said with a half wave.

'Fires really are the most challenging but intriguing of crime scenes, aren't they?' Amis stated.

'I suppose they are,' French replied with a confused frown and then gestured to the body. 'Can we have a look?'

Amis pulled a face. 'Not very much to look at I'm afraid. And pretty unpleasant. It almost put me off my breakfast this morning.'

Almost? Garrow thought dryly.

'Can you tell us if the victim is male or female?' Garrow asked.

'Your victim is male,' Amis said. 'My instinct is that it's a young man.'

French arched his brows. 'How young?'

'Not a teenager.' Amis wiped some sweat from his brow. 'But I'd say under thirty.'

'Is there anything else you can tell us that might help to identify the body?' Garrow enquired. 'We have two relatively young men unaccounted for who both work in the holiday park.'

'Oh right… I'm very sorry.' Amis shook his head. 'Unless something suddenly turns up in the forensics or the preliminary post-mortem, then I'm afraid we're going to have to rely on DNA. And that's going to take a bit of time.'

Garrow gave French a look of frustration.

They needed to get DNA material from a toothbrush, comb etc… for both the missing men. And then, even if they fast tracked the DNA samples, it could take between twenty-four–forty-eight hours before they could make an identification.

CHAPTER 13

Nick glanced across CID which was now a hive of activity as witness statements, evidence and the initial forensics from the holiday park were being scrutinised. French and Garrow had returned from Colwyn Bay about half an hour earlier. A large scene board had been set up with temporary photos of both Kevin Ball and Matthew Hopkins.

The photo of Kevin Ball showed him as a small, diminutive man in his late twenties with scruffy blond hair and slightly protruding teeth. He had a drink in his hand and was raising it to whoever was taking the photograph. Parallel to that was a photo of Matthew Hopkins. He was handsome, with olive skin and a mop of black curly hair. The photo was a selfie that showed Matthew grinning and doing the peace sign.

'Right guys,' Nick said as he strolled across the CID office. 'At the moment, there isn't anything that I can add to the information about the boss's condition. She is critical but stable. As a temporary measure, she has been placed in an induced coma to allow her brain and body time to heal.' Nick left a suitable silence as he approached the scene board. He could feel that his words had created a collective worry in the room. However, there was nothing to be done but to move on with the investigation and keep busy. 'Okay... At the moment, we have an unidentified victim who has perished in a fire in a cabin at the Pen-y-Bryn Holiday Park close to Colwyn Bay. Our priority is to identify that person as quickly as possible so that the next of kin can be made aware.' Nick then pointed to the two photos. 'And we have two men in their twenties who are missing or unaccounted for at the park. Professor Amis' initial assessment is that the victim is a young male, so we are assuming that one of these men could be our victim.'

French looked over. 'But it might be neither of them,' he suggested.

'Yes, that's true.' Nick nodded. 'And until we have DNA confirmation, then we can't conclude anything. But I do think it would be an extraordinary coincidence if our victim turned out to be someone else.'

'Boss, I've spoken to forensics,' Garrow said as he sat forwards in his seat. 'They have collected DNA samples for both Kevin and Matthew. And from the victim. But it is going to take them up to twenty-four hours to analyse these and see if they can get a match.'

'Thanks, Jim,' Nick said, unable to hide his frustration. Even though he knew that forensics would be working as fast as they could, he seemed to spend a huge amount of his time waiting for their results before decisions about an investigation could be made. 'The chief fire officer believes that the fire might have originated in the car that was parked beside the cabin.'

Garrow looked up from where he was taking notes. 'Are we going on the theory that our victim wasn't targeted? That their death was accidental?'

'Correct,' Nick agreed. 'Where are we at with finding the details of the car and its owner?'

French pointed to his computer screen. 'Just got an email from the DVLA based on the VIN number that forensics found.'

A phone rang and Garrow answered it.

'Go on,' Nick said.

'It was a silver Renault Megane,' French stated and then looked at Nick. 'Registered to Kevin Ball. And the registered address is Pen-y-Bryn Holiday Park.'

Nick raised an eyebrow. 'What is Kevin Ball doing with a shotgun in his car?' He wondered if the gun and the car being burned was connected to Kevin Ball's disappearance.

Garrow indicated the phone. 'Boss, that was Professor Amis. Something has come up in the preliminary post-mortem and he'd like to show us.'

'Okay,' Nick said, hoping it was something that would give them a breakthrough in identifying their victim. 'You and Dan get over to the mortuary and see what it is. I'm going to head over to the holiday park to see if there's anything there we've missed and talk to the chief fire officer. Everyone else, scrutinise the statements of everyone who was at the park last night. Did anyone see anything suspicious or out of the ordinary? Did anyone see our two missing persons? And can we chase any CCTV that the holiday park has from last night?'

CHAPTER 14

French and Garrow were inside the lift at the Llancastell University Hospital heading down to the basement where the mortuary was located.

'Did you hear back from Mold Crown Court about Lucy Morgan?' French asked as the lift descended with a loud clunking noise.

Garrow had been trying not to think about it. 'Yes. She's pleaded not guilty. Trial is set for the end of August so she'll be on remand until then.'

Garrow could feel his pulse quicken every time he thought or talked about Lucy Morgan. He was feeling very anxious about what she was going to say about their 'relationship' during the investigation into her mother's murder. Although nothing romantic had ever happened between them, there was no doubt their conversations had crossed the line and had been inappropriate. He wished he'd listened to French when he'd warned him that he was getting too close. And he had no idea if Lucy was going to make allegations against him that weren't true.

French nodded as the lift reached the basement and the doors juddered open noisily. 'Don't know why, but it still amazes me that people will commit murder over the contents of a will.'

'Accursed greed for gold, to what dost thou not drive the heart of man,' Garrow said.

French looked none the wiser. 'Okay.'

'It's Virgil,' Garrow explained.

'From the *Thunderbirds*?' French asked.

'What?' Garrow looked puzzled. 'No, the Roman poet and philosopher.'

French just rolled his eyes as they approached the double doors to the mortuary and pushed them open.

'What?' Garrow asked defensively.

As soon as the doors opened, a wave of cold air hit Garrow's face along with the smell of disinfectants and preserving chemicals.

Amis pulled down his green surgical mask and gave them both a smile as though they had just met on a golf course for a quick round.

'Here they are again,' he laughed.

'Ah, Llancastell's answer to *Quincy*,' French joked. He had clearly planned this as a retort to Amis' usual jokes based on television police shows.

'Touché,' Amis guffawed. 'You really are showing your age now Sergeant.'

'I think they were repeats,' French replied with a dry smile.

'Yeah, I think I do vaguely remember it,' Garrow admitted with a frown. 'American TV series about a coroner?'

'A medical examiner,' Amis corrected him. 'But essentially the same. Jack Klugman was the actor. I first saw him in *Twelve Angry Men* with Henry Fonda.'

Garrow nodded. He had seen the film. It was a classic. 'Directed by Sidney Lumet. Great director,' he said.

Amis turned his head to French and grinned. 'It appears that you're working with a cinephile, Sergeant.'

French shrugged and shook his head. 'I have literally no idea what you two are on about.' He then pointed to the burned body that was over on the metallic gurney. 'You wanted to show us something?'

'Cause of death is what you would suspect,' Amis said. 'Smoke inhalation. Technically, he died from asphyxia caused by synergistic toxicity from carbon monoxide and other irritant gases.'

French looked a little irritated. Garrow knew that Amis wasn't telling them anything useful, or anything that couldn't have been relayed via a quick phone call.

'You said there was something "interesting" that you'd found?' French said, trying to hurry Amis along.

'Oh yes,' Amis said with a guffaw. 'Of course. A couple of things actually. The toxicology report showed that your victim had sodium oxybate in his bloodstream. More commonly known as Gamma-Hydroxybutyric Acid.' Amis gave them a look as if that should mean something.

Then Garrow twigged. 'GHB?'

'Correct,' Amis said and then joked. 'Starter for ten, no conferring.'

GHB was a party drug that produced a feeling of euphoria, relaxation, sociability and sometimes sexual arousal. However, in higher doses it could cause dizziness, sleepiness and even unconsciousness, which meant that it was also used as a 'date rape drug'.

French raised an eyebrow. 'Enough to render the victim unconscious?'

Amis thought for a moment. 'I'm afraid that our tests aren't accurate enough to tell us that. However, I did also find high levels of alcohol in the blood samples. Mixed together, I would guess that your victim would have been feeling pretty out of it.'

'Can you tell how it was administered?' French asked.

'No,' Amis replied. 'Your victim might have taken the drug as part of their night out. But it often comes as a liquid so it's easy to slip a few drops into someone's drink.'

Garrow looked over at French. If someone had spiked either Matty or Kevin's drink, had they also intended for them to die in the fire in Cabin 5?

'You said there were "a couple of things", Tony?' French prompted Amis.

'That's right. Your victim also had a severe accident at some point in his life. Their right leg has several pins, rods and screws where both the femur and tibia were shattered. Despite the intense heat of the fire, the pins and rods are made from a titanium alloy which can survive the heat.'

'Any idea when the accident might have happened?' Garrow asked.

'After your victim was fully grown,' Amis replied. 'The position of the rods and pins suggests there had been no growth after they were inserted.'

French looked at him. 'And this would have been a pretty serious accident?'

Amis nodded. 'It would have taken him several months to be able to walk normally again.'

Garrow shared a look with French. This might be significant in identifying their victim before the DNA results proved conclusive.

CHAPTER 15

As Nick sped towards Pen-y-Bryn Holiday Park, he saw a sign to *Llandrillo-yn-Rhos – Rhos-on-Sea*, a seaside resort to the north of Colwyn Bay. He had visited Rhos-on-Sea many times as a kid. As a Welsh history enthusiast – even as a boy – he remembered visiting the Llandrillo-yn-Rhos church. There had been a church on the site since the sixth century, which Nick thought was incredible. The church that sat on the site now was a mish-mash of structures from the thirteenth, fourteenth and eighteenth centuries.

However, the thing that excited Nick the most about Rhos-on-Sea was the story of Madog Owain Gwynedd. According to Welsh folklore, Madog, a Welsh prince, set sail for the Americas in 1170 from Rhos-on-Sea, a whole three hundred years before Christopher Columbus. It was claimed that the Welsh sailors landed at Mobile Bay in Alabama and then made their way up the Alabama River. They intermarried with the local Native American Cherokee tribes and helped design and construct stone forts which bore a similar design to Dolwyddelan Castle in North Wales.

When eighteenth century explorers came to the area, they found Welsh influence along the Tennessee and Missouri Rivers. A tribe called the Mandan told stories of how 'white men' built their towns and villages with streets and squares. The Mandan also spoke a language which incorporated the Welsh language, and they fished the rivers in coracles, the boat of Ancient Wales, rather than traditional canoes. The most compelling argument came from the Governor of Tennessee who wrote a report in 1799 mentioning the discovery of six skeletons that wore armour bearing the Welsh coat of arms.

Being a fierce and proud Welshman, this proved to Nick what he had always known. The Welsh were a far stronger, intelligent and capable race of people than they had ever been given credit for.

Turning left off the main road, Nick was still preoccupied by those thoughts as he took the road which weaved through the holiday park. He parked up close to the area where other emergency vehicles were parked and got out. The air was still thick with the bitter smell from the burning shell of the cabin over to his right.

Heading for the police cordon, he pulled out his warrant card and showed it to the young female officer who was supervising a few onlookers and holidaymakers.

'DS Nick Evans, Llancastell CID,' he said. 'I'm looking for Sergeant Robinson.'

'Yes, sir,' the female officer said and pointed. 'She's over there.'

'Thank you, constable,' Nick replied, as he made his way towards Robinson who was talking to a smartly dressed man in his fifties. From Jim and Dan's brief description, Nick assumed it was Miles Hopkins, the owner of the holiday park.

'Sergeant Robinson?' Nick asked as he approached and showed his warrant card. 'Mr Hopkins?'

'Miles, please,' Hopkins said quietly. The stress of not knowing if his son had perished in the cabin fire was clearly getting to him. He looked drawn and slightly lost.

'DS Evans,' Robinson said. 'We've got the chief fire investigator down here now. There have been a couple of significant developments that I think will impact your investigation.'

'Okay,' Nick said, wondering what she was referring to. 'Can I speak with him?'

Robinson pointed to a giant of a man in his fifties, dressed in fire retardant clothes, gloves and a yellow helmet. 'That's him over there. Huw Davies.'

Nick walked over and pulled out his warrant card again. 'Huw Davies?'

'Yes,' he replied in a deep voice with a strong North Wales accent.

'DS Nick Evans. I understand you've found something significant?'

'Yes, that's right,' Davies replied with a serious expression. He then pointed to the area which would have been the front of the cabin. 'We've found traces of an accelerant on what we think were the steps and the door to the cabin.'

'Any idea what it might have been?'

'My guess is petrol,' Davies replied. 'Your boys in forensics should be able to narrow it down, but I'd be surprised if it wasn't.'

'And that means that the fire originated on the steps and the door to this cabin?' Nick asked. 'We were led to believe that it was a car fire that was the cause?'

'Now we've found the accelerant, we've had to reassess that original theory, I'm afraid,' Davies explained. 'It seems that the car ignited because it was parked next to the cabin.'

Nick took a moment. If Davies was correct, the investigation might have just moved from being one of manslaughter to murder.

'And there's no other explanation for what you found by the steps and door?' Nick asked to clarify. 'It's not something for treating the wood or some kind of cleaning fluid?'

'No,' Davies replied defensively. 'Whatever it was, it was highly flammable. We've seen enough arson cases to know what we're looking at.'

Nick could see that Davies didn't like his assessment to be disputed. 'Look, I know you guys are experts in this field. It's just that if someone poured petrol on the steps and door to this cabin, we might be looking at a murder case.'

'That's your call,' Davies replied, still a little frosty. 'My job is to give you our opinion based on what we find and what we can see.' He then gave Nick a dark look. 'If you follow me, there is something else I'd like to show you.'

'Of course,' Nick said as he trod carefully over some patches of burned grass.

Davies stopped by various pieces of wood that had been deliberately laid out on the ground beside the red fire investigation van. He then crouched down and showed Nick part of the door with its metallic handle and lock.

'We've managed to retrieve most of the cabin door, its handle and lock,' Davies explained. 'We also found a key inside the lock on the outside.' He then looked up at Nick. 'The door to the cabin had been locked from the outside. Presumably once the victim was inside.'

Nick's eyes widened.

Okay. Now we definitely have a murder case on our hands.

CHAPTER 16

Hammersmith Odeon

29 October, 1983

The crowd outside the Hammersmith Odeon was growing. Ruth, fourteen years old, and her two class-mates, Vicky Clarke and Claudia Temple, had been queuing for ninety minutes for the Wham! Fantastic Tour gig. Ruth was beyond excited. She was wearing black ribbons in her hair just like Madonna, along with white boots, a dark pink ra ra skirt and a denim jacket.

Some of the girls started to chant 'We want Wham!' but just as they had started the large double doors to the Hammersmith Odeon opened. There was a surge of high-pitched screams as teenage girls lurched forwards, showed their prized tickets and then sprinted inside.

Ruth and her friends got to their seats which were about six rows from the front. She couldn't believe their luck.

'This is bloody ace!' Claudia squealed breathlessly.

Grabbing her pink *Le Clic* camera, Ruth shouted, 'Let's get a photo of all of us with the stage in the background!'

She looked around and identified a middle-aged woman behind them with two girls whom she assumed were her daughters.

'Excuse me,' Ruth said to her politely. 'Would you mind taking our photo?'

'Course not, love!' the woman said with a smile as she took the camera and lined it up. 'Squeeze in a bit, girls,' she laughed, gesturing with her hands. 'That's it. Now say cheese.'

Ruth and her friends all said 'Cheeeeeese' in unison.

'There you go,' the woman said, handing back the camera.

'Aw thanks,' Ruth said gratefully as she took the camera and manually wound the film on ready for the next shot. She had a roll of twenty-four photos and she fully intended using the whole roll during the concert.

Vicky began to look through the glossy A4 Wham! Fantastic Tour Souvenir Programme. It basically featured photos of the band.

She put her hand on Andrew Ridgeley's bare chest on one photo and swooned. 'Oh my God, he's sooo brown.'

They all giggled.

'He's much better looking now he's had those blond bits put in his hair,' Claudia said as she chewed pink bubble gum like her life depended on it. The others agreed.

After an hour of a well-known DJ called Gary Crowley playing various soul and rare groove records the house lights went down.

There was an ear-splitting scream which made Ruth put her fingers in her ears for a second.

Her heart was pounding with excitement. She could hardly get her breath.

The opening bars to the song *Bad Boys* started to play and there was more screaming. The bass seemed to reverberate through her whole body. It was so loud.

George Michael entered stage right wearing a yellow Fila sports top and shorts. Simultaneously, Andrew Ridgeley came on from stage left wearing a red Fila sports top and shorts.

Although it didn't seem possible, the screaming got louder and the air seemed to crackle with the overwhelming noise.

Ruth winced at the noise but couldn't help but give a deafening squeal of excitement.

Pepsi and Shirlie, the Wham! backing singers and dancers, appeared at the back of the stage to more screaming. Ruth became aware that she got a funny feeling when she looked at Shirlie. She'd noticed it when she'd seen Wham! on Top of the Pops. Shirlie was so cool, with blonde hair and piercing green eyes. And she was so sexy when she danced.

After a few songs, there was an interval.

Ruth's ears were ringing and it felt like someone had stuffed them with cotton wool. A screen appeared on the stage and a series of childhood photos were shown. A young George Michael with very curly hair and glasses. Andrew in his pyjamas.

'I was so excited when they came on stage, I nearly bloody wet myself,' Vicky admitted.

'I can't believe that we're actually this close to them,' Claudia squealed, gesturing to how near the edge of the stage was. 'I just want to touch Andrew's legs.'

The second half was greeted by another crescendo of screaming. George Michael sang a beautiful song that he said he'd written when he was only sixteen called *Careless Whisper* that no one had heard before. Then came *Love Machine, Young Guns* and *Nothing Looks The Same In The Light*.

The whole thing ended with an upbeat disco track *Come On*. George and Andrew had pretended to play a game of badminton with rackets and shuttlecocks. Andrew wiped the sweat from his forehead onto a shuttlecock and then hit it into the crowd to huge screams. George did the same. Then Andrew licked the end of another shuttlecock and hit it right towards where Ruth and her friends were sitting.

Ruth watched the shuttlecock loop into the air and head straight for her, almost as if it was in slow motion. Reaching up, she instinctively caught it.

Looking at her friends in astonishment, Ruth jumped around with the shuttlecock in her hand.

'I caught it! I caught it!' she yelled.

CHAPTER 17

As Nick strode across the holiday park, his phone rang. It was French.

'Boss,' he said with an urgent tone.

'What did Amis have to say?' Nick asked immediately.

'Victim has GHB in his bloodstream, but he can't tell us the amount, so it could have been taken recreationally…'

'Or someone could have deliberately spiked his drink,' Nick said.

'Exactly.'

'Anything else?'

'Metal pins and rods which survived the fire were found in the victim's right leg,' French said. 'Amis said that at some point in his adult life, the victim had a fairly serious accident. It would have put him in hospital for a reasonable amount of time and taken a few months to recover from.'

'Okay,' Nick said, taking in this new information. 'I'll see if I can track down either Miles or Jane Hopkins. See you later.'

Nick ended the call and spotted a man in a green Pen-y-Bryn Holiday Park waterproof jacket and black baseball cap. As he got closer, Nick saw that the man had a badge – *Dylan Williams – Manager.*

Taking out his warrant card, Nick looked at him. 'I'm looking for Miles Hopkins,' he explained.

Williams pointed to a long one-storey building over to the right. 'Last I saw him, he was sitting at the bar,' he said, pulling a face. 'Have you managed to find out who was in the cabin yet?'

'I'm afraid I can't divulge anything about the investigation until we have confirmation and have spoken to the victim's next of kin,' Nick stated.

'Yeah, of course,' Williams said quietly. 'It's just horrible. Kevin and Matty are good blokes and… well, you know.'

'Of course,' Nick said empathetically. 'We'll let everyone know as soon as we have anything significant.'

'Thanks,' Williams said as he turned and walked away.

Nick walked over to the building and into the holiday park bar. He saw that Hopkins was sitting on his own in the far corner nursing a very large whisky. Even though Nick was in recovery and had no interest in drinking alcohol, he could completely understand why Hopkins was drinking to deal with the stress. He couldn't imagine how agitated and upset both he and Jane must be not knowing the fate of their son.

'Miles,' Nick said quietly as he came over. Even though he had delivered terrible news to relatives many times, he knew that he might be about to confirm that it had been Miles' son Matty who had died in the fire. 'I'm DS Nick Evans from Llancastell CID. Mind if I sit down?'

Hopkins looked very anxious. 'Have you identified who was in there?'

Nick pulled out a chair, sat down and said in a low voice, 'We have had some information from the chief pathologist which we believe is significant in making that identification. So, I just need to ask you a couple of questions, if that's okay?'

Hopkins nodded but seemed to freeze with fear. 'Of course,' he said very quietly.

'Can you tell me if Matthew was ever in a serious accident?' Nick asked.

The blood drained from Hopkins' face. He nodded. 'Yes,' he whispered.

Nick looked at him. 'And was his right leg severely damaged in that accident?'

Hopkins didn't reply but nodded. It was clear that he now knew it was his son who had died inside the cabin.

After a few seconds of silence, Hopkins' eyes filled with tears and he took a long, deep breath. 'Yes. Matty was involved in a moped accident about three years ago. His right leg was badly injured and he had to have it pinned back together.' Hopkins looked at Nick. 'I don't know why I didn't think of that before. I could have told you.'

Nick gave him an empathetic look. 'I'm really sorry.'

'It's him, isn't it? It's Matty,' Hopkins said almost to himself as he wiped a tear from his face and took a long, deep breath.

'What you've told me does fit with what the pathologist found,' Nick said gently.

Hopkins lifted his whisky. His hand was shaking as he took a long swig.

'I... I must find Jane and tell her,' Hopkins stammered.

'Jane?' Nick asked. 'That's Matty's mother?'

'Stepmother,' Hopkins said, and shook his head. 'I'm afraid Matthew's mother died when he was very young. Jane has always been there for him and he calls her mum.' Then the shock overwhelmed him. 'Oh God, what are we going to do?'

Out of the corner of his eye, Nick spotted a middle-aged blonde woman walking across the bar towards them.

Although he wasn't certain, he thought it was probably Jane Hopkins.

'Kevin Ball has turned up,' the woman said to them as she arrived at the table completely flustered. 'He's in a hell of a state. I think he's broken his ankle. He stinks of booze.'

There was an awkward silence.

She could clearly sense that something was up.

Nick pulled out his warrant card. 'DS Nick Evans…'

'What is it?' she asked anxiously, interrupting him.

'Jane, I think you should sit down,' Hopkins said in a sombre tone.

'What is it?' she asked again as the panic set in. Her eyes roamed nervously around the room. She looked at Nick. 'Do you know something?'

Hopkins got up from the table and placed a comforting hand on her shoulder. 'It was Matty who was in the cabin.'

'No, no…' Jane shook her head. 'We don't know that yet. Just because Kevin has turned up…'

'I'm really sorry,' Nick said, speaking softly. 'Our pathologist found the pins and rods in the victim's right leg…'

'From the accident,' Hopkins whispered.

'No, please no,' Jane cried as she dissolved into tears. 'There must be a mistake.'

Hopkins put his arms around her as she sobbed. 'It isn't a mistake.'

'Oh God,' Jane sobbed as she buried her face in Hopkins' chest.

Spotting that the bar staff and customers were looking over, Nick glanced at Hopkins. 'Is there somewhere a little quieter or private we can go?'

Hopkins' eyes were also full of tears now. 'Yes. We can go to my office.'

'Thank you,' Nick said as he took out his phone. While he dealt with Matthew's parents, he needed Jim and Dan to interview Kevin Ball asap to find out where he'd been and why he'd been missing.

CHAPTER 18

Nick had been sitting in Miles Hopkins' office for about ten minutes. Jane was sitting on the sofa next to her husband just staring into space and holding a tissue. Every couple of minutes, she would dissolve into tears and he would try to comfort her.

Holding his notepad, Nick had taken down all the formal details that he needed. He knew that he now had to broach the subject of Matthew's death possibly being deliberate.

'I'm afraid I do have something else distressing to talk to you about,' Nick said gently.

Jane looked apprehensively at Hopkins.

'I don't understand,' Hopkins said, leaning forwards with a frown.

'We are going to be treating this death as murder,' Nick explained. 'I'm so sorry to have to tell you that.'

'What?' Hopkins gasped, narrowing his eyes in disbelief.

'No, no,' Jane protested. 'It was an accident. I don't know why you're saying that.'

'I've spoken to the chief fire investigator,' Nick said in a soft, low tone. 'There is evidence that an accelerant was used to start the fire on the steps and by the door of the cabin. Most likely petrol.'

Hopkins and Jane looked at each other aghast.

'We also found evidence that the door had been locked from the outside,' Nick stated. 'The key was still in the lock but on the outside.'

'God,' Hopkins muttered, shaking his head. 'Who would do that?'

Jane's face was twisted as she took in the news. 'That just doesn't make any sense.'

'The toxicology report also showed traces of a drug called GHB,' Nick explained. 'Although we can't be certain, it is possible that Matthew was deliberately drugged last night.'

'Drugged?' Hopkins said under his breath.

'What if they didn't know Matty was inside the cabin?' Jane muttered as if she was almost talking to herself. 'It could have just been an accident.'

'Can you think of any reason why anyone would want to burn down that cabin?' Nick asked. They couldn't completely rule out Jane's theory, but Nick's instinct was that this was a deliberate attack and that Matty was the intended target.

'No,' Hopkins admitted. 'But the cabin was supposed to be empty. No one knew that Matty was in there.'

'I'm assuming that someone saw Matthew go into the cabin,' Nick said, trying to be as tactful as he could. 'They then locked him inside and set the cabin on fire. It's the only logical explanation I can find for the key being on the outside of the door and the door being locked.'

'Why?' Jane gasped as she wiped her face and nose. Her hands were both visibly shaking. 'Why would someone do that to him?'

Nick took a moment and then said gently, 'I was hoping you might be able to help me with that.'

'Matty didn't have an enemy in the world,' Hopkins protested immediately.

'He wouldn't have hurt a fly.' Jane furrowed her brow and then sobbed. 'Everyone loves Matty. He's the life and soul.'

'Could you tell me if you noticed any change in Matty in recent days, or even weeks?' Nick asked. 'Was there anything worrying him? Did he get into any arguments? Anything out of the ordinary?'

'No, nothing,' Jane whispered. 'I can't believe that anyone would want to hurt Matty.'

Hopkins paused for thought as though something had occurred to him. Nick noticed.

'Please. Anything, however small you think it is, might help us,' Nick said encouragingly.

'Matty and Kevin did have a falling out about ten days ago,' Hopkins admitted.

Jane looked confused. 'That was just some silly argument over Kevin's terrible timekeeping.'

Hopkins looked at her and then over at Nick. 'To be honest, I thought it was more than that. In fact, it seemed that Kevin was angry with Matty rather than the other way around.'

'How serious did it get?' Nick asked, now thinking that this might be significant.

'Just a bit of pushing and stuff,' Hopkins explained. 'I had to pull them apart.'

Jane's eyes widened. 'What?'

'I didn't tell you,' Hopkins said with a shrug. 'I didn't want to worry you. I just thought it was young men having a bit of a row that's all.' He looked over at Nick. 'I really don't think that Kevin would have had anything to do with this.'

Nick wasn't so convinced. They needed to talk to Kevin Ball as soon as possible.

CHAPTER 19

Garrow and French had just arrived at the holiday park and were now making their way through towards the static caravans where some of the staff lived. Garrow glanced over at Matty Hopkins' caravan where they'd been only a few hours earlier. Events were changing fast in the investigation.

They spotted a dishevelled-looking man in his twenties sitting smoking a vape on the steps of a caravan on the opposite side. He was small, with a mop of blond hair and slightly protruding teeth.

Garrow recognised him from the photograph they had on the scene board in the CID office.

'Kevin Ball?' asked French, as he pulled out his warrant card and approached him.

The man nodded but immediately looked worried. There was a cut on his temple and his clothes were stained. His ankle was heavily strapped. Even from where Garrow stood, he got a very strong waft of alcohol.

Jesus, it smells like it's coming out of every pore, he thought.

'Is Matty still missing?' Ball asked, as he blew out a cloud of vape and rubbed his hand through his hair.

Garrow noticed that his hands seemed red raw on the palms.

'Can you tell us where you were last night, Kevin?' French asked.

'I wish I bloody knew. I was hammered,' Ball snorted. 'Can't remember a thing. Is this to do with the fire up at that cabin?'

A girl in her early twenties – dyed pink hair, piercings, black baggy clothes – appeared.

'Who the fuck are you?' she snapped at them.

'Coppers,' Ball said.

'You found Matty yet?' she asked.

Wow, she's delightful, Garrow thought to himself dryly.

'And you are?' French asked calmly.

'Kat,' she replied.

'Kat?' French asked as he took out his notepad. He looked at her to indicate that he wanted her full name.

'I'm not giving you my bloody name,' she growled. 'I know my rights.'

'Fucking hell, Kat,' Ball groaned, shaking his head. Then he looked at them. 'It's Kat Mount. Katherine.'

'You dickhead, Kev,' Kat snarled.

'Thank you,' French said as he wrote down her name in his notepad.

Kat glared at Kevin. 'Yeah, and where the fuck were you last night? 'Cos I wanna know too.'

Ball shrugged with an ironic smile. 'Wish I could tell you, babe.'

'Yeah, it's not funny. You need help. You're a bloody alcoholic,' Kat snapped before turning, heading inside the caravan and slamming the door.

'Sorry about her,' Ball said with a grin.

French locked eyes with him. 'I'm going to need you to tell me everything you can remember from last night.'

French's mobile phone rang and he answered it.

Ball narrowed his eyes and glared at Garrow. 'Shouldn't you lot be out there looking for Matty?'

Garrow didn't answer.

French ended the call and looked over at Ball. 'Kevin, I'm going to need you to accompany us to the station. Anything you do say may be used in a court of law. I'm also going to need the clothes you were wearing last night.'

Ball gestured to the clothes he was wearing. 'I haven't even had a shower or changed yet.'

'Come on,' French said. 'Let's go.'

'Are you arresting me?'

Garrow moved towards him. 'We can explain everything when we get to the station.'

Ball got wearily to his feet.

Kat appeared at the door. 'Oi, where do you think you're taking him?'

'Llancastell Police Station,' French replied.

CHAPTER 20

An hour later, Nick and French made their way down the back stairs as they headed for Interview Room 2. For a moment, Nick's thoughts turned to Ruth. It felt like there was a horrible black void in his life. Ruth was godmother to his and Amanda's daughter Megan. It dawned on him that if anything happened to Ruth, or if she didn't come out of the coma, he would have to try to explain it to Megan. It would break her heart as she was close to her 'Auntie Ruth'.

French's phone rang which broke Nick's train of thought.

French answered it as they went. 'DS French?... Right, thanks for letting me know.' He ended the call.

Nick gave him a quizzical look.

'That was the forensics lab,' French explained. 'The DNA from our victim is a match for Matty Hopkins.'

Nick nodded. Even though they had been working on the assumption that it had been Matty who had been killed, there was always a tiny element of doubt – until now.

'I'll have to go and let Miles and Jane Hopkins know after we finish with Ball,' Nick said, thinking out loud.

They arrived at Interview Room 2 on the ground floor and went inside.

Ball was dressed in a grey sweatshirt and bottoms. He stared solemnly at the wall. The duty solicitor, Amanda Price, forties, blonde, wearing a smart navy suit, was sitting beside him. A duty solicitor was an independent criminal defence solicitor from a local Llancastell law firm who represented anyone suspected or accused of committing a crime who didn't have legal representation.

Nick and French went over to the table.

'Morning,' Nick said politely to Price.

'Morning,' she replied quietly as she looked at the documents in front of her.

'Are we all ready?' Nick asked.

Price looked at Ball and then nodded.

Nick leaned over and pressed the red button on the digital recording equipment. There was a long, loud electronic beep.

'Interview conducted with Kevin Ball, Interview Room 2, Llancastell Police Station. Present are Duty Solicitor Amanda Price, Detective Sergeant Daniel French, and myself, Detective Sergeant Nick Evans.'

Nick glanced over at Ball. 'Kevin, do you understand that you're under caution?'

Ball narrowed his eyes and gave a nonchalant shrug.

Nick was trying to suss him out but he couldn't seem to get a handle on him. He couldn't work out if his defiant, belligerent behaviour since his arrest was just a big act. Sometimes suspects overcompensated for their fear with bad behaviour. Others really just didn't give a damn.

French sat forwards and looked at him. 'Can you tell us where you were last night, Kevin?'

Nick and French had agreed that at this stage of the investigation it was prudent not to tell Ball that Matty

Hopkins had died in the cabin fire. That allowed them to hit him with that information and see how he reacted.

Ball gave an audible huff. 'I told you all that in the car on the way here.'

'Well this is a formal interview which we are recording,' French explained calmly. 'So, I'd like you to tell us again.'

'I got off work about six. Went for a couple of drinks at the bar,' Ball stated.

French, who was now taking notes, looked up. 'And that's the bar at the Pen-y-Bryn Holiday Park in Colwyn Bay?'

'Yeah.'

'And you work at the park, is that correct?' he asked.

Ball nodded. 'Yeah, I run the bike hire for the park.'

'And how long have you been working there?'

'Three years,' he replied.

Nick sat forwards on his chair. 'Okay, take us through everything you can remember from last night please.'

Ball rolled his eyes. 'I went for a few drinks at the bar with some of the staff. Then I got a text from Layla.'

French frowned and stopped writing. 'Layla?'

'Layla Hughes,' he said.

'Does Layla Hughes work at the park?' Nick asked.

Ball shook his head. 'Not anymore. I went to school with her. She was up here with some friends who work here, celebrating her birthday.'

'Okay,' French said. 'Go on.'

'They were sitting out drinking by the fire pit, so I sat with them for a while,' he explained. His manner had started to soften a little.

'And how long were you there for?' French enquired.

'Few hours.'

'How many of you were there?'

'Five or six. It was just girls. And then I left them to it.'

'What time do you think that was?'

'Gone midnight.'

Nick frowned and then pointed to the burns on his right hand. 'Can you tell us how you got those burns on your hand?'

'I don't understand why you're asking me all this,' he snapped. 'Why aren't you out there trying to find Matty?'

Nick fixed Ball with a stare. 'Please answer the question, Kevin.'

'As I was walking back, I saw that one of the cabins was on fire,' he explained. 'I'd parked my car next to it because no one had booked it. But I saw my bloody car was on fire. I ran over to try and put it out and...' he lifted up his right hand, '...this happened.'

'Did you see anyone around the cabin at that time?' French asked.

'Miles Hopkins was up there. He was on his phone trying to get help.'

Nick took this information in for a moment. They needed to check where Miles Hopkins lived and establish how he'd got on site and up to the cabins first.

Nick looked at him. 'Can you tell us why you had a shotgun in the back of your car?'

'It's my dad's,' Ball replied uneasily. 'He's got a licence for it.'

Nick frowned. 'That's not what I asked you, Kevin.'

'I was doing a bit of rabbit shooting in the fields near the holiday park with some mates a few weeks ago,' he said. 'I forgot to take it back.'

French looked at him. 'You do know that it's an offence to keep a firearm in your car? Your dad could have his licence cancelled.'

Ball rolled his eyes. 'Yeah, well I'm gonna have to buy him a new bloody gun now.'

After a few seconds, Nick asked, 'You said that you'd tried to put the fire out in your car. So, what did you do then?'

'I watched my bloody car go up in flames for a bit, but there was nothing I could do about it. I was fucked off so I went down to my caravan, grabbed a bottle of vodka and went off and drank it on me own. Then I woke up this morning.'

'You didn't try to help put out the fire in the cabin?' Nick asked.

'Nothing I could I do.' Ball shrugged. 'And the fire brigade were on their way so...'

Nick thought it was strange that Ball had decided to walk away from the burning cabin and car, down to his caravan and then drink himself unconscious. It didn't ring true.

'Apart from Miles Hopkins, did you see anyone else around the cabin?' he asked.

Ball shook his head. 'No. Some of the holidaymakers had come out of their cabins to see what was going on. Most people were keeping their distance.'

Nick nodded, waited for a few seconds and then sat forwards in his seat.

'How would you describe your relationship with Matty Hopkins?' he asked.

'I dunno.' Ball shrugged. 'We're mates I suppose.'

'So, you're close friends?'

'No,' he said defensively, as he shifted uncomfortably in his chair. 'I wouldn't say that.'

Nick frowned.

'Matty tends to spend most of his time with girls,' Ball said in a knowing tone. 'If you know what I mean?'

Nick and French shared a look.

'Do you mean he sleeps around?' French asked to clarify.

'Yeah, he's like a dog with two dicks. In fact, that's probably where he is right now. Shacked up with some girl.'

Nick noticed Ball's response was in the present tense. If he was involved in Matty's murder, he was doing a good job of hiding it and throwing them off the scent.

'I understand that you had a fight with Matty a few weeks ago that Miles Hopkins had to break up?' Nick said. 'Can you tell us what that was about?'

'Nothing really,' Ball said with a nonchalant shrug. 'Matty kept on about my timekeeping. I just told him to fuck off as he wasn't my boss. It wasn't anything serious.'

Nick held his gaze. 'Are you sure? Miles Hopkins seemed to think that it was more than that?'

Ball shrugged. 'No. Matty's the boss's son so he likes to throw his weight around. It gets up some people's noses, you know. It's not like anyone can say anything to Miles is it?'

Nick nodded. It was probably time to hit Ball with the truth of what they knew and see how he responded.

He looked over at him. 'I'm afraid I've got some bad news for you. Matty was discovered inside the cabin that burned down… He's dead.'

'What?' Ball looked like he'd been punched in the face. He then shook his head. 'That doesn't make any sense.' His eyes roamed around the interview room for a few seconds as he processed what Nick had said. 'What the hell was he doing in there?' he said in a virtual whisper.

'We don't know yet,' Nick replied. 'Do you know why he might have been in there?'

'No,' he answered, still in shock. 'God, that's horrible. I...'

French looked over from where he was making notes. 'When was the last time you saw Matty?'

'I saw him last night,' Ball admitted, still stunned by what they had told him. 'He was sitting with Layla and her friends by the firepit.'

French narrowed his eyes. 'Why didn't you tell us that before?'

'You didn't ask,' he replied defensively.

Nick rubbed his jaw and said, 'And was Matty at the firepit when you left?'

'No.'

Nick frowned. 'Do you know where he went?'

Ball hesitated.

'Whatever it is...' Nick said in a serious tone, '...you do need to tell us.'

Ball looked concerned. 'Matty went off with Layla.'

'Where did they go?' French asked.

'They headed off towards the woods. But there's no way that Layla is involved in this.'

'Do you know why they were going to the woods?' French enquired.

'I think they might have been cutting through the woods to go back to Layla's flat.'

'Do you know why they were going there?' French asked.

Ball furrowed his brow and snorted, 'Why do you think?'

'Did you see Matty after he'd gone off with Layla?' Nick said.

'No.' Ball shook his head sadly. 'That was the last time I saw him.'

CHAPTER 21

Garrow and French had tracked Layla Hughes down to a small café just off the West Promenade in Colwyn Bay. As they parked on the seafront, Garrow looked out at the vast expanse of sand that stretched for almost as far as the eye could see both ways. The spring sunshine had burnt most of the clouds away and the sky was a beautiful azure blue.

The beach was inhabited mainly by people walking their dogs. A young couple walked hand in hand with a black Labrador running nearby. The man tossed a large stick along the beach close to where Garrow and French had parked. The dog skittered away across the wet sand. Even though Garrow felt uncomfortable admitting it, he was a little jealous of the couple. He hadn't had a serious girlfriend since he was at university, and the idea of walking hand in hand down a beach, tossing a stick for a dog, seemed very appealing.

'You look miles away,' French said as they got out of the car.

Garrow didn't respond. He felt a little embarrassed that his daydreaming had been so obvious.

Striding across the main road, they came to a traditional-looking café called *The Bay Café*. It had a red and white awning and swirly gold writing on the large glass window.

They went inside where simple black wooden chairs and tables were laid out. The walls were painted a very light fawn and large framed photos of Colwyn Bay were dotted around. A blackboard listed toasted sandwiches, Welsh cakes and scones on the menu.

An attractive woman with a ponytail and dark makeup approached. 'Table for two is it?' she asked. She had a Geordie accent.

French and Garrow pulled out their warrant cards.

'DS French and DC Garrow, Llancastell CID. We're looking for a Layla Hughes,' French said discreetly.

'That's me,' she replied, looking instantly anxious. 'Is something wrong?'

'Just a couple of routine questions, that's all,' Garrow reassured her. 'Won't take a minute.'

'Is it about that fire up at the holiday park?' she asked as she nervously pushed a strand of hair from her face. Her hair was bleach blonde with dark roots underneath.

Garrow looked at the customers in the café. 'Is there somewhere a bit quieter we could go?' he asked softly.

Layla nodded but now she was looking very worried. 'There's a little room out the back we could go to?' she suggested, gesturing to a door.

'Thanks,' French said. 'Let's go in there, shall we?'

'I just need to tell my manager that I'm going in there,' Layla murmured as she walked briskly over to a middle-aged woman in an apron behind the counter, before returning.

Garrow and French followed Layla across the café, through the door and into a small office. There were a couple of plastic chairs on one side. On the other was a desk, computer, an office chair and shelves that were stacked with box files.

'Shall we sit down?' Garrow suggested.

Layla nodded but her eyes showed how scared she was.

'We understand that you were celebrating your birthday up at the holiday park last night?' French said.

'That's right,' she replied.

Garrow pulled out his notepad and pen. 'Can you tell us what your relationship is to Matty Hopkins?'

Layla's eyes widened. She looked gobsmacked by the question.

'Relationship?' she said with a frown. 'I don't have a relationship with Matty. Why? Has he told you that I do?'

Garrow looked at her. 'But you were with him last night?'

Layla didn't reply for a few seconds but moved a strand of her hair off her face nervously.

'Yeah,' she said defensively. 'I mean he was sitting with me and my friends having a drink and that.' She gave them a quizzical look. 'Can you tell me what this is all about? Is he all right?'

'We have a witness who saw you leave your group of friends with Matty, is that right?' French asked.

This question also rattled her. 'I dunno what you're talking about,' she said unconvincingly.

French raised an eyebrow. 'Are you telling us that you didn't go anywhere with Matty Hopkins last night?'

'Aye, we sloped off for a bit,' she admitted. 'Is Matty all right? Has something happened to him?'

'Can you tell us where you went and what you were doing when you "sloped off"?' Garrow asked.

'I don't think I want to tell you what we were doing.' Layla pulled an angry face. 'I don't think it's any of your business.'

French gave her a serious look. 'I'm sorry to tell you that Matty Hopkins died in that fire at the holiday park last night in suspicious circumstances. We're trying to find out where he was and what he was doing, so it is our business I'm afraid.'

The blood drained from Layla's face. 'Matty's dead?' she gasped, her face now revealing her shock.

'Yes. I'm sorry,' Garrow said gently.

Layla shook her head and then took a breath. 'Oh God...' Then her eyes filled with tears. 'Sorry, I... I can't believe it.' She wiped her face with the back of her hand and sniffed. Then blinked as she looked at them, the mascara had started to run from her lashes. 'Sorry...'

'That's okay,' French said now with an empathetic look. 'But we do really need you to tell us what you were doing with Matty last night right up to the point when you last saw him.'

Layla nodded, took a tissue from her pocket and wiped her eyes. 'We went back to my flat,' she said under her breath. 'I was driving.'

'Where is your flat?' Garrow asked.

'Upstairs.' Layla gestured to the ceiling. Her flat was clearly above the café.

French looked at her. 'Had you been drinking?'

Layla shook her head. 'I don't drink.'

French gave her a quizzical look.

'My parents were alcoholics,' she said as way of an explanation. 'It put me off for life.'

Garrow looked up from where he was scribbling in his notepad. 'We do need you to tell us what happened when you got back to your flat,' he said with a respectful tone.

Layla took a deep breath and then eventually said, 'We had sex.'

Garrow nodded, making sure that he didn't change his facial expression due to her answer. 'And was that the first time that you and Matty had had sex?'

'No.' Layla shook her head but then the grief seemed to overwhelm her. She took another deep breath as she wiped the tears from her eyes again.

'It's okay,' Garrow reassured her. 'Take your time.'

'We'd slept together a few times. But we weren't together or anything like that,' she said with a sniff. 'But I really liked him. I can't believe he's dead.'

French looked at her. 'Do you know if Matty had a regular girlfriend?'

'No.' Layla shook her head and gave them a forced smile. 'Matty wasn't interested in having a girlfriend.'

Garrow picked up on her comment and squinted in confusion. 'Do you mean that he slept around a lot?'

Layla gave a slight nod. 'He wasn't horrible or aggressive or anything like that,' she explained adamantly. 'It's just that he was a bit of a free spirit. That's what women found attractive in him.'

Garrow nodded and then pointed to his notepad. 'Do you know when Matty left your flat?'

'About eleven, maybe,' she suggested.

'Do you know where he went?'

'He said he was going to walk back to the park. It's only about ten minutes if you cut across country and go through the woods.'

'You didn't go with him or drive him?' Garrow enquired.

Layla shook her head. 'I had work this morning.'

'And he didn't say anything about where he was going or what he was going to do when he got back?' French asked.

Layla didn't reply for several seconds. She clearly had something on her mind.

'Please,' Garrow said gently. 'Whatever it is, it might help us find out who did this to Matty.'

'He went to get some flake,' Layla said.

'Cocaine?'

Layla nodded but she was clearly uncomfortable telling them this.

'Where was he going to get the cocaine from, Layla?' French asked.

Layla took a breath. 'Kat... Kat Mount.'

CHAPTER 22

Half an hour later, French and Garrow were back at the holiday park. Garrow looked up and noticed that the weather had changed quite suddenly. A dull slate-like colour had replaced the clear blue of the sky. The branches of the trees were bent back and heaved like sails in the strengthening wind, their leaves hissing as they scraped across each other.

They approached the static caravan where Kat lived with her boyfriend Kevin Ball. The door to the caravan was open and loud dance music was blaring.

French knocked on the open door. 'Anyone in?'

Kat appeared and her face instantly turned to a sneer. 'What do you want?'

French gestured to the inside of the caravan. 'Okay if you turn the music down a bit?' he said loudly over the din.

Kat shrugged and signalled to her ears. 'Can't hear you,' she shouted.

Jesus, we've got our work cut out here, Garrow thought to himself as French glanced over with a forced smile.

Then French lost his patience and went to step inside the caravan.

Kat stood in his way. 'You're gonna need a search warrant if you want to come in here,' she snapped.

'Turn the music down... PLEASE!' French growled.

Kat smirked, went off and turned the music off.

Thank God for that!

'Right, you've already harassed Kev,' Kat groaned. 'What do you want?'

Garrow looked at her. 'Can you tell us the last time you saw Matty Hopkins?'

She took a moment and then replied, 'Dunno. Yesterday some time.'

'You work at the park?' French enquired.

'Yeah. Doing the changeovers,' Kat said defensively. 'Strip the beds, change the towels.'

Garrow had taken out his notepad. 'Can you tell us what time you saw Matty yesterday?'

'No.' Kat gave a surly shrug. 'Couldn't tell you exactly.'

French frowned. 'You didn't see him last night then?'

She narrowed her eyes suspiciously. 'No. I didn't see him last night,' she said emphatically.

French looked at Garrow with a mock look of confusion.

Garrow raised a doubtful brow. 'Matty Hopkins didn't come to this caravan last night?'

'No,' Kat huffed. 'I've just told you that.'

'And you're sure about that?'

'Bloody hell!'

Garrow took a moment as he narrowed his eyes and gave her a quizzical look. 'We were led to believe that Matty did come to this caravan last night. Just before midnight?'

'Who the fuck told you that?' Kat demanded angrily.

'We're not at liberty to divulge that information I'm afraid,' French explained calmly. 'In fact, we've been informed that Matty came here to purchase cocaine. Is that correct?'

'Cocaine?' Kat snorted with derisive laughter. 'For fuck's sake! You've been watching too many films.'

'That's not true then?' Garrow asked.

Kat took a visible breath as her brow furrowed. 'You deaf or something? Matty didn't come here last night. And I don't sell "cocaine"'.

French gestured to the caravan. 'Mind if we come in and have a look around?'

Kat shrugged. 'If you've got a search warrant,' she said with swagger.

'Actually, we're conducting a murder investigation,' French said in a serious tone. 'And if we believe that we need to enter your caravan as part of our investigation, we don't need a search warrant.'

Kat frowned as she weighed up what French had said for a moment.

Suddenly, she charged out through the door, knocking French flying. She sprinted away down the holiday park.

'Jesus,' French gasped holding his side. Then he gestured. 'Go after her... I'll call for back up.'

Garrow turned and broke into a run.

He raced down past the static caravans.

Kat was about fifty yards ahead of him. She turned to check and saw that he was chasing after her.

With his arms pumping, Garrow hit his stride. He wondered what the connection was between Kat selling Matty drugs and his death. Was there one? Had she done a runner because she was selling drugs, or for a darker reason?

Kat darted right and cut down past the last caravan in that part of the holiday park.

Garrow followed her just as a middle-aged man came out of his caravan holding a mug of tea and a plate of toast.

'Jesus!' the man yelled, as he jumped out of the way as Garrow thundered past – the tea and toast went flying.

'Sorry!' Garrow called back without breaking his stride.

As he looked up, he saw that Kat had started to climb up a steep, grassy embankment. The effort meant that she was no longer able to run. She looked around but when she saw Garrow heading her way she clearly realised that she had no choice but to plough on up to the top of the slope.

Garrow was running flat out and his shoes were beginning to rub against his heels. He could feel the sweat running down his forehead and back.

Twenty yards to go.

Kat glanced back down the slope at him. Her escape had slowed to a lumbering walk as she gasped for breath.

'Stay there, Kat!' Garrow yelled.

Surely she could see she wasn't going to get away.

Ten yards.

His lungs were starting to burn with the effort as he sucked in air.

'Kat, just stop there!' he gasped. 'You're not going anywhere.'

'Fuck off,' she said.

She then took a step, lost her balance and came rolling down the embankment for a few seconds.

'For fuck's sake,' she shouted as she tried to get up again.

A moment later, Garrow was on her. He grabbed his cuffs, pulled her hands behind her back and cuffed her.

'Katherine Mount, I'm arresting you for assaulting a police officer,' he panted.

'Get off me you paedophile,' Kat screamed.

'You do not have to say anything, but it may harm your defence if you do not mention, when questioned, something which you later rely on in court. Anything you do say may be given in evidence.'

CHAPTER 23

December 1997

Lighting a cigarette, Ruth leaned back against the wall to the rear of Lavender Hill Police Station. She blew a plume of smoke out into the cold air and looked down at her uniform. She couldn't help but feel relief that this might be the last time she would ever have to wear it. It was her last day working as a constable at Lavender Hill nick. Next week she was transferring to Peckham to begin work as a detective constable in CID. She felt a mixture of fear and excitement at the prospect.

Glancing at her watch, she saw it was ten a.m. Even though she had been through the same morning routine, it had a different significance today. Since passing out from the Hendon Police Training College in July 1993, Ruth had worked as a PC in Battersea. She was a Battersea girl, born and bred. It was her 'manor'. So, it had been mixed blessings when she had started to pound the streets of SW11 as a probationer. Her knowledge of the local area and some of the 'faces' had proved invaluable. However, her grandfather and dad's reputations as petty criminals, combined with some locals' pre-conceived ideas about the dysfunctional nature of 'The Hunter Family', sometimes hindered her work. And moving across to Peckham, SE15, was going to be a breath of fresh air, a new start, and that's why she couldn't wait.

Having changed in the female locker room, Ruth had sat through her last briefing and rota assignments from Sergeant Ackroyd. In her books, Sergeant Ackroyd was all right. Tall and gangly with milky skin, he was a gruff cockney on the outside, but he cared about the job and treated everyone the same. The fact that Ackroyd had four daughters, whom he loved to bits, also made him one of the good guys in the station. The same couldn't be said for many of his male colleagues. When she had arrived as a probationer, there were still male police officers who would try it on and get her to make them cups of tea or do other menial tasks. Some had called her *love*, *Doris* or *plonk* – 'person of little or no knowledge'. It wasn't quite the dark days of the seventies, but their misogyny was revolting. There were still the infantile sexual innuendoes and the odd slap or grope.

'Thought I'd find you skulking out here,' joked a voice.

It was Ackroyd.

'Sorry, Sarge,' Ruth said as she dropped the cigarette to the floor and stubbed it out with her shoe.

'Last day, eh?' he said with a chuckle, but there was something about his manner that suggested he was feeling uncomfortable.

'How did your daughter get on with that audition?' Ruth asked. Ackroyd had told her, while they were out on patrol the previous day, that his daughter Michelle had gone for an audition for a small part in the television soap *Eastenders*.

'Yeah, she got the part,' he replied with obvious pride. But she could see that there was something else still troubling him.

'Everything okay, Sarge?' she asked, looking at him.

'Yeah,' he said, rubbing his hands together. 'Brass monkeys out here, isn't it? Let's go in, eh?'

Ruth nodded. 'Yeah. As it's my last day, I'll treat you to a coffee from the canteen.'

Ackroyd pulled a face. 'Not really a treat, is it?'

'No,' Ruth laughed as they headed towards the door to go back inside.

Ackroyd then stopped. 'Actually there is something.'

Ruth stopped. 'Okay?'

'I don't know how to put it really,' he admitted. Whatever he was struggling with, it was making him feel very uneasy.

'Okay,' Ruth said gently.

'My daughter Michelle,' he said. 'I think she's…' Then he gestured with his head as if to indicate she would know exactly what he meant.

Does he mean he thinks that she's gay?

Ruth frowned. 'Erm…'

'I think she's… a… queer,' Ackroyd whispered.

'I think we say "gay" these days,' Ruth said, trying to hide her bemusement.

Ackroyd nodded. 'Oh right.'

Why is he telling me this?

Ruth raised an eyebrow. 'Does it bother you?'

Ackroyd thought for a moment. 'Not really. I want her to be happy, that's all. It's not easy out there being… gay, is it?'

His comment struck a chord with Ruth. Even though she had a long-term boyfriend, she had had several 'encounters' with women over the years. Most of them had been when she was very drunk. A gay male friend of hers just shrugged and said 'It just means that you're bisexual.'

Ruth wasn't sure that was it. She had always noticed that she was more attracted to women if she was really honest with herself. Maybe it was her upbringing or her job that prevented her really taking a look at her true sexual preference.

'No, it's not,' she agreed as they headed back into the station. 'Actually…'

Ackroyd stopped and looked at her. 'Yes?' he asked.

'Erm, I've got a female friend who's gay,' Ruth said. 'She says that it's getting easier and easier these days to be open about that sort of thing. Maybe you shouldn't worry too much, eh?'

'Oh right. That's good to know.' Ackroyd nodded. He looked vaguely relieved. 'Come on. If you're buying, I'm gonna have a round of toast too.'

CHAPTER 24

Garrow and French had debriefed Nick on what had happened at the holiday park and Kat's arrest. French was suffering from no more than mildly bruised ribs.

Nick leaned over and pressed the red button on the digital recording equipment. There was a long, loud electronic beep.

'Interview conducted with Katherine Mount, Interview Room 2, Llancastell Police Station. Present are Duty Solicitor Amanda Price, Detective Sergeant Daniel French and myself, Detective Sergeant Nick Evans.'

Kat was now dressed in a grey sweatshirt and bottoms. She glared at them across the table as she bit at the sides of her nails.

Nick glanced at her. She wasn't doing herself any favours. 'Katherine, do you understand that you're under arrest for the possession of Class A drugs with intent to supply?'

Once Kat had been arrested, the SOCOs were called in to do a forensic sweep of the caravan. They had found twenty grams of what their tests showed was cocaine.

Kat gave a nonchalant shrug. 'My name's Kat. Only person who called me Katherine was my mum and she's dead.'

Legally, Nick still needed Kat to confirm that she understood that she was under arrest. If the interview was used as evidence, he didn't want a canny defence barrister trying to get the interview struck off on a technicality.

The duty solicitor, Price, leaned in and whispered something to Kat – presumably telling her to answer his question.

Rolling her eyes, Kat huffed. 'Yes, I understand.'

French sat forwards on his chair, reached over and opened a file. 'For the purposes of the tape, I'm showing the suspect Item Reference 382F.' French took a photograph and turned it to show Kat. 'Can you tell us what you can see in this photograph?'

Kat gave the photograph of a twenty-gram bag of cocaine a furtive look. 'No comment.'

Great, thought Nick. He had hoped that Kat wasn't going to give them a 'no comment' interview, even though they were becoming increasingly common.

'Our forensic officers found twenty grams of cocaine in your caravan, Kat,' French continued. 'Is there anything you can tell us about that?'

Kat looked down at the floor with a bored expression. 'No comment.'

Nick looked over at her but she didn't make eye contact. 'Does the cocaine belong to you?'

'No comment.'

'Do you know what the sentence is for possession and intent to supply Class A drugs?' Nick asked calmly.

Kat didn't answer.

Nick glanced over at French. 'DS French, what do you think the sentence might be for possession and intent to supply twenty grams of cocaine?'

French took a moment to think. Then he looked over at Kat. 'The last person we prosecuted for this kind of offence got eight years.'

'Eight years,' Nick said under his breath. 'That's a long time to be locked up.'

Kat seemed to react to their comments. Her foot was now jigging nervously.

'Can you tell us where you got your cocaine?'

There was silence but Kat was staring intently at the floor. All the anger, bravado and self-assurance had gone. She bit the edge of one of her nails.

'It's not my flake,' she whispered.

'Sorry?' Nick said, leaning forwards. 'I didn't quite catch what you said there.'

Kat glanced up at him, looking dejected. 'I said, it's not my coke.'

Nick raised an eyebrow and asked, 'Whose coke is it then?'

'No comment,' Kat replied.

'The problem is,' French said, 'the cocaine was found in your caravan. And I'm pretty sure we're going to find your fingerprints on that gram bag. So unless you can tell us whose cocaine it is, then we're going to assume it's yours. And so will a judge and the court.'

'It's Kev's,' Kat muttered under her breath as she looked down at the floor.

Nick glanced at French. Even though their main focus was finding out who had murdered Matthew Hopkins, they needed to process the cocaine possession.

'The cocaine belongs to Kevin Ball?' Nick asked. 'Is that correct?'

'Yes,' Kat whispered unconvincingly. Clearly the stress of implicating Ball was getting to her.

'For the purposes of the tape, I'm showing the suspect Item Reference 823J,' French said as he pulled out another document. 'This is a statement given to us by Kevin Ball earlier today.' He turned the document for Kat to look at but she hardly gave it a glance.

Nick looked over at her. 'In his statement, Kevin Ball claims to have come back to the caravan that you share with him at around midnight. He told us that he retrieved a bottle of vodka from the caravan and then went off to drink it alone and that's the last thing he remembers.' Nick pointed to the document. 'Kat, did you see Kevin when he came back to the caravan last night?'

She shook her head. 'No.'

Nick shot French a look. If she was telling the truth, then Kevin Ball had lied about his whereabouts last night. And that was definitely suspicious.

Nick raised an eyebrow quizzically. 'Are you sure?'

Kat nodded in annoyance. 'Of course I'm sure.'

'So, you would have been awake at around midnight when he came back?' French enquired.

'No,' Kat replied. 'I had to have an early night. The changeover starts at six a.m. for some of the cabins and caravans. I was asleep by eleven.'

Nick looked confused. 'Then how do you know Kevin didn't come back?'

'I locked the caravan door. I always do,' she explained. 'But Kev had forgotten his keys. I didn't know that until he knocked on the door at dawn this morning. He couldn't have come back because he couldn't get in.' Kat looked at them. 'Plus we didn't have any vodka anyway. I don't know what he's talking about.'

Nick exchanged a look with French. Kevin Ball had lied to them.

CHAPTER 25

Nick wandered slowly down the hospital corridor holding a bunch of flowers and a large packet of Wispa chocolate bars. He had already been over to the ICU to check on Ruth. Ella was there but there was little to report. Ruth was still in an induced coma. Despite the brain scans, the doctors just didn't know what damage the cardiac arrest had done. And they wouldn't know until they were sure that it was safe for them to bring her slowly out of the coma.

The air was thick with the smell of hospital food and disinfectant. He held open the door for a young man in a wheelchair with a drip attached to his arm. He noticed that he was missing his left leg.

'There you go,' Nick said.

'Thanks, mate,' the young man said in a thick North Wales accent.

Nick gave him a kind smile. 'No problem.'

A few seconds later, Nick entered the ward where he knew Georgie was recovering from the accident and her ordeal.

Looking into the ward, he immediately spotted her. Her face lit up when she saw him. There had been a time when he and Georgie had been very close. Probably too close. And Georgie had been very clear that she was attracted to him. However, she seemed to have mellowed, and he now counted her as a friend, as well as a valuable work colleague.

'Hey,' Georgie said as she sat up in the bed. Then she spotted the Wispa chocolate bars. 'You remembered?' she cried in delight.

'Of course.' Nick knew that they were her favourite. Then he gave her a meaningful look. 'Have they said anything about how long you'll be in here?'

Georgie nodded. 'Could be discharged as early as tomorrow.'

'Really?' Nick didn't like the sound of that. 'Don't they need to observe you for a bit longer?'

'Apparently not,' she replied brightly. 'Baby is doing well. All I've got is a bit of concussion and a badly bruised shoulder and arm. I can be back to work in a few days.'

'Woah, slow down there, Tonto,' Nick said, putting his hand up in concern. 'You were kidnapped at gunpoint and knocked unconscious in a car crash. *And* you're pregnant. You need to rest and fully recover before you even think about coming back.'

Georgie didn't reply but looked a little vulnerable. Nick worried that something he'd said had made her feel uneasy. 'Sorry, I didn't mean…'

'No, it's fine,' she reassured him, but something was making her feel uncomfortable.

'I didn't mean to be heavy handed,' Nick said gently.

'If I'm honest, I don't want to be stuck at home on my own,' Georgie admitted, and then pointed to her head. 'If I'm stuck with this thing all day, it's going to drive me mad. And when I'm at work, I'm busy and distracted, and that makes me feel safe.'

'Yeah, I understand,' Nick stated. 'I know exactly what you mean. When I was on the run and in that prison cell I took stock of everything. I had a lot of thinking time. And of course I missed Amanda and Megan. It was horrible. But I also missed "the job".'

'Exactly,' Georgie agreed. 'It's all I can think about. Getting back to work.'

Nick looked at her. It was hard to describe to *a civilian* what it meant to be a police officer. The buzz, the camaraderie and the overwhelming sense of giving something back and helping people when they were often at their most vulnerable and desperate. It was like nothing else.

'If you're coming back, it's desk duty only,' Nick said as a compromise.

'Great.' Georgie's expression brightened. 'DS Nick Evans, I could kiss you,' she laughed.

'Yeah, I don't think that's a good idea,' Nick said with a raised eyebrow as he thought of the couple of *near misses* they'd had in the past.

Georgie narrowed her eyes. 'Don't flatter yourself. I don't fancy you anymore.'

Nick grinned. 'Yeah, you say that…'

Georgie pointed to the packet of chocolate bars. 'You can fuck off now you've brought me chocolate.'

'Charming,' Nick snorted. 'You are aware that technically I'm currently your commanding officer?'

'Jesus, God help us all,' Georgie joked. 'Okay. You can fuck off now you've brought me chocolate, *sir*?'

He laughed and shook his head. 'Yeah, that's much better,' he said dryly.

CHAPTER 26

Ella and Sarah were back at the ICU, sitting either side of Ruth's bed. Now that she had been placed into a temporary induced coma, Ruth had a ventilator pipe taped to her mouth to help her breathe.

Sarah's mind was whirring as she stared vacantly at Ruth on the bed. She was lost in thoughts and memories. She felt overwhelmed by feelings of guilt and regret. The years they had lost together when Sarah had disappeared. Even though, logically Sarah knew that her disappearance wasn't her fault entirely, deep down she was aware that it had been her behaviour that had put her in such a vulnerable position.

In 2013, Sarah and Ruth had been living together as a couple in their flat in Crystal Palace, south-east London. Sarah boarded a train to London Victoria one morning and vanished. What Sarah hadn't told Ruth was that she had become secretly embroiled in the seedy world of elite sex parties in London through a man named Jamie Parsons.

A few days before she had vanished, Sarah had witnessed Lord David Weaver raping and then 'accidentally' killing a teenage girl in a bedroom at one of these *Secret Garden* sex parties. Lord Weaver was a life peer who had served as both foreign secretary and chief whip in the late 1980s. He was a very visible member of the House of

Lords, often photographed with the great and the good, the rich and the famous. His wife Olivia moved in social circles with lesser members of the royal family.

To make matters worse, Sarah's presence in the room had been spotted by Jamie Parsons and three others. Jurgen Kessler, a German banker and close friend of Parsons, who was wanted by Berlin Police for questioning in connection to the murder of two young women. Patrice Le Bon, a multimillionaire owner of several Paris model agencies, who was under investigation for human trafficking. And Sergie Saratov, a Russian billionaire, who had gone underground when police investigated his extensive use of escorts and sex workers in hotels that he owned in an exclusive European ski resort. These men were very rich, very powerful, and therefore very dangerous. And Sarah was an eyewitness. She was taken away to France and was forced to move around Europe for the next few years working as a high-class escort. It had now been nearly two years since Ruth had flown to Paris and rescued Sarah from the clutches of Global Escorts. Nick, Sarah and she had nearly lost their lives.

Effectively, Sarah and Ruth had lost seven years together. However, once Sarah had moved to North Wales, they got their relationship back on track, and that lost time didn't seem to matter as much. They had the rest of their lives together.

Until now…

The young doctor with glasses came into the room holding some files. It broke Sarah's train of thought. She immediately searched his face to see if he was about to give them important news. The results of some test they had done or one of the many scans. Every time the door opened, Sarah's stomach clenched and her pulse quickened with anxiety. Most of the time it was just a nurse who would check Ruth's blood pressure, pulse and the ECG reading before giving them a kind smile and leaving the room again.

The doctor didn't say anything as he gave Ella and Sarah a cursory glance and headed over to Ruth to check on the ECG reading.

Sarah and Ella shared a nervous look.

Opening one of the files, the doctor looked over at them. 'I do have some good news. This morning we carried out a coronary angiogram. One of the major blood vessels to Ruth's heart was blocked so we have addressed that with a stent.'

Ella sat forwards. 'Do you know how long you're going to have to keep her in the coma?'

The doctor thought for a second. 'I'd like to see how she reacts to having the stent fitted.'

Sarah nodded but sighed, almost to herself, 'I just want her to be at home.'

The doctor gave them a serious look. 'A cardiac arrest is very serious. I think you need to prepare yourselves for a long recovery time. And you might find that Ruth has some personality changes. She might have issues with her memory and her speech. And she might be irritable, tired and just not seem like herself.'

Sarah frowned. Part of her would take Ruth back however she was. But part of her wanted everything to go back to the way it was a few days ago. 'How long will she be like that?'

'No way of telling. Days, months.' He then narrowed his eyes. 'Sometimes the neural damage is permanent and those changes are permanent.'

Sarah felt her whole body react to this news. She felt sick.

CHAPTER 27

It was nearly eight a.m. the following morning as Nick sat back on Ruth's chair and looked at the paperwork that was piling up on the desk. Despite the digital age with computers and email, it was incredible how much paperwork a murder investigation produced for the senior investigating officer to look through. There were overtime sheets and requests to sign off on. Witness statements to read through and scrutinise. The SIO also had to authorise any significant requests for forensics, mobile phone and bank records, as well as applications for CCTV footage or access to the North Wales Police automatic number plate recognition software and cameras.

Blowing out his cheeks, Nick sipped his coffee and rubbed his eyes. Glancing outside he could see that the CID team were assembling for the morning briefing. Then he looked back at the files. If he was going to progress from DS to DI, he was going to need to get used to dealing with the more tedious side of police investigations.

He stood up, stretched, grabbed his coffee and strode out into the CID office. Usually, once a crime had become what was deemed *a major incident*, the team would relocate to the major incident room. However, budget cuts to the North Wales Police meant that IR1, as it was known, was now being used by the child protection team.

Nick didn't mind, although, IR1 had more space and specialist equipment for a major incident. But there wasn't anything he could do about it so there was little point in dwelling on it.

'Right everyone,' he said as he made his way towards the scene board. 'I'm afraid I have nothing new to report about the boss. But her daughter Ella and her partner Sarah wanted me to pass on their thanks for the lovely flowers and card that you guys sent. It's much appreciated.' Nick waited before feeling that it was appropriate to now move on with the briefing itself. He then pointed to a photo. 'Okay, we know that Matty Hopkins was murdered but at the moment we're struggling to find any obvious prime suspect. Dan?'

French got up, came over to the board and pointed to two photos. 'We have Kevin Ball and Katherine Mount. Katherine has been charged with possession of Class A drugs with intent to supply. She has been released on bail pending a trial date.' French pointed again. 'My instinct is that these two are somehow mixed up in this. Ball has minor burns to his hands where he claims he tried to extinguish the fire in his car. He also lied to us about going to his caravan to retrieve a bottle of vodka just after midnight. The fact that he lied to us is suspicious. We also have the altercation between Ball and Matty which Miles Hopkins had to break up. Ball claimed it was a petty argument over his poor timekeeping, but Miles Hopkins thought that it seemed more serious than that and that Ball was the instigator of the fight.'

'Do we believe Kat Mount's allegation that the cocaine we found belonged to Ball?' Nick asked.

'My instinct was that she was lying,' French said.

'Me too,' Nick agreed. 'But my instinct is that they're both hiding something.'

Garrow looked over. 'We've got the toxicology report on Matty. It shows traces of alcohol and GHB, but not cocaine. That means that Matty didn't go to the caravan to buy cocaine, so Kat is not lying about that.'

'Good point,' Nick said. 'Okay. Do we have any sign of Matty's mobile phone?'

'I've got the digital forensics team trying to triangulate the signal,' Garrow explained.

Nick nodded. 'What about CCTV for the park?'

French gestured to his computer monitor. 'I'm just trawling through it now.'

Nick went over to the detailed map of the area that was on the far left of the scene board. 'Let's contact traffic and pull any CCTV from the surrounding area. From the looks of it, Dolwen Road is the only road that you can access the park from. Let's look at any CCTV we can get both north and south of there. I want a log of all cars going up and down that road between ten p.m. and one a.m.'

'I was thinking about the petrol, boss,' Garrow said.

'Go on,' Nick said.

'The chief fire investigator said that someone used a substantial amount of petrol to light the fire at the cabin,' he continued. 'There are only two petrol stations in the area, and they both had CCTV on the forecourt. Maybe they've spotted someone filling up cans of petrol in the last week?'

'Good point,' Nick agreed. 'Go and have a look. How are we getting on with the forensics on Kevin Ball's clothing?'

'Still waiting,' Garrow replied.

'Fingerprints or forensics on the key we found in the door?'

'Forensics think they might get a print, but any useful forensics would have been destroyed by the fire,' Garrow explained.

'Have we got anything on the witness statements from staff or holidaymakers?' Nick asked. 'Did anyone see anything suspicious around that cabin? Anyone lurking around?'

A phone rang and Garrow picked it up.

French shook his head. 'I've been through them. No one seemed to see anything until after the fire started.'

Garrow looked over at Nick. 'Boss, digital forensics want you to go over so they can show you something.'

'Okay, good work everyone,' Nick said as he headed back to the Ruth's office to collect his jacket.

CHAPTER 28

Ten minutes later, Nick had crossed the road to the new forensics building and was now sitting with a digital forensics officer. The room comprised two rows of state of the art computers facing each other. Above these were black shelves that contained audio and digital tracking machinery, which glowed and made low humming noises.

The female officer – twenties, spiky blonde hair, glasses – pointed to the digital map of Colwyn Bay on a large monitor mounted on the wall. 'I think we've just had a breakthrough, sir,' she said as she pushed her glasses up the bridge of her nose. 'If I can show you?'

'Go for it,' Nick said as he approached the monitor.

'Okay, this was our problem here,' she said, high-lighting an area of Colwyn Bay and the Irish Sea.

'Problem?' Nick asked.

'Because of the sea, the mobile phone signal is weak in this area because there aren't enough cell towers. So, at first, we could only narrow down Matthew Hopkins' mobile phone to the Colwyn Bay area. Which obviously isn't particularly helpful.'

'No,' Nick agreed.

'However, I rang the number just over an hour ago and someone picked up the phone and then hung up,' she explained.

'Okay,' Nick said, now intrigued.

'That then registered on these two cell towers here and here,' she said, pointing to the monitor. 'We've managed to triangulate the phone to this address here,' she explained as she clicked a button to zoom into the map.

'Any idea what that is?' Nick asked as he peered at the map. It was an address on a side road close to the beach.

'It's registered to a flat above *The Bay Café*,' the female officer explained.

Layla Hughes.

CHAPTER 29

Garrow and French made their way towards the coast. Garrow gazed out at the countryside to his left. The spring sunshine was bright and the trees that lined the roadside cast shadows so deep that they appeared a bluish black across the road itself. As the line of trees stopped, an uneven dry stone wall took its place. Beyond that were endless meadows full of sheep munching on fresh grasses and wild flowers.

Some movement from a large pond in the distance caught Garrow's eye. A huge bird with a dark brown body and beautiful jade-coloured wings rose majestically into the air with a wingspan of two to three feet.

'Wow,' he said under his breath. 'That's a green heron.'

French glanced over as the heron flew high into the sky. 'Bit of a twitcher are you? Doesn't surprise me.'

'Not really,' Garrow said. 'My dad was. Every time we went anywhere in the car, he would point out various birds as we went along and give all the details.'

'That sounds nice,' French stated. 'The only thing my dad ever pointed out when we were driving along were pubs. And then we'd stop. He and my mum would sit at the bar in silence and I'd be stuck outside with a bottle of pop and a packet of crisps. If you did that now, they'd call bloody social services.'

'The good old days, eh?' Garrow smiled.

'Not that you'd know much about all that,' French teased him.

'Too young and too posh?'

'Exactly.'

'I did try to swat up on birds so I could join in with my dad on our drives,' Garrow admittted. 'But then I realised that he loved to be the fountain of all knowledge. He didn't want me chipping in every five minutes and stealing his thunder.'

French pointed to something up ahead. It was the petrol station they had identified as being the closest to Pen-y-Bryn Holiday Park. Indicating left, French pulled the car off the main road and onto the forecourt. A red tractor was filling up with diesel on the far side.

Getting out of the car, Garrow saw a big blue sign – *Croeso – Welcome* that was rocking slightly in the wind.

They headed across the oil-stained forecourt and entered the shop which was empty. A young man in his early twenties – stocky with a patchy blond beard – was standing behind the till stacking vapes onto a shelf.

As they approached, he turned to greet them with a friendly smile.

They pulled out their warrant cards and his face fell.

'Okay if we ask you a couple of questions?' French said politely. 'Just routine.'

'Erm, yeah,' he replied, blinking nervously.

Garrow looked at him. 'You work here every day?'

He nodded. 'Yeah.'

'We're looking for anyone who might have come in here and filled up several cans of petrol in the last few days,' Garrow explained.

The young man frowned for a second. 'We've had a couple of people filling up one can. But I can't remember anyone… Hang on.' He tried to remember. 'There was someone.'

'Any idea who it was?' French asked.

'No,' he replied, still deep in thought. 'I'm pretty sure it was last Thursday because it was really hot that day. And we have a thirty litre limit on customers who fill up petrol cans. I think it came to just over twenty litres but I remember making a note to check it. I can't remember much about the customer I'm afraid.'

French looked at the monitor behind the tills and pointed. 'You've got CCTV though, haven't you?'

'Oh yeah,' he said, pulling a face. 'Didn't think of that.'

'Mind if we have a look?' French asked.

'No, of course not.' He opened the door and allowed French and Garrow to come into the area behind the tills.

He then turned around and went to the machine beside the monitor. 'CCTV from Thursday should be on the hard drive here,' he explained as he tapped away at the keyboard.

'How long do you keep your CCTV?' Garrow asked.

'We've been told to erase it at the end of every month unless something has cropped up that needs looking at. Here we go.'

Garrow leaned forwards and saw the CCTV footage of the forecourt from Thursday. The young man began to play it forwards at high speed until he spotted something. 'I think this is it,' he said brightly.

The footage showed a green Land Rover Challenger pulling up beside a pump. A figure got out of the car wearing a baseball cap. They went to the boot of the car, took out four petrol cans and began to fill them.

French peered intently at the screen.

'There,' he said. 'Can you play that back and pause it for us?'

Garrow went closer to the screen and looked as the footage played again.

The figure who was filling up the cans turned and looked up.

Garrow immediately recognised him. He looked at French.

'Yeah, that's Miles Hopkins,' French said to him.

Garrow nodded, pulled out his phone and took a photo of the screen.

CHAPTER 30

Having checked inside the café, Nick had established that Layla Hughes wasn't due to start work until after lunch. He went outside and pressed the buzzer that had *Flat 1a* scribbled beside it.

'Hello?' said a woman's voice after a few seconds.

'I'm looking for Layla Hughes,' Nick explained calmly.

'Erm... Yes... That's me,' Layla replied.

'It's DS Evans from Llancastell CID,' Nick said in a light, calm tone. 'I need to ask you a couple of routine questions. It won't take more than a few minutes.' He didn't want to alert her as to why he was there, or the gravity of what the digital forensics team had discovered.

There was no reply, but a few seconds later there was the metallic sound of keys unlocking a door.

The front door opened and Layla gave him an uncertain look. She had delicate features with a curvy mouth. Her hair was curled and rested loosely on her shoulders. There was a velvety brown mole, or beauty spot, on her cheek which gave her face added prettiness. She was wearing an oversized black hoodie, joggers and Adidas slides.

'Layla?' Nick asked.

'Yeah.' She nodded and gestured for him to follow her up the carpeted stairs to her flat. 'Do you want to come in?'

'Thanks.'

Nick went up the stairs and entered the small one-bedroom flat. It smelt of washing powder and he could hear the sound of a washing machine.

Layla looked at him uncertainly and gestured to an open door. 'We can go in here if you want?'

Nick gave her a nod and followed her into a compact living room. Layla went over to a black leatherette armchair. On the other side of the room was a sofa covered in a thin flower-printed throw which had been tucked down into its back. Nick sat down and looked around for a moment.

The room was cluttered. Makeup was scattered across a coffee table, and there were coffee cups and crumb-strewn plates on the carpet next to a pile of magazines.

Nick looked at her. 'I understand from my colleagues that you were with Matty Hopkins on Saturday night at the Pen-y-Bryn Holiday Park. And then you came back here. Is that right?'

Layla nodded. Her body language was closed and she chewed nervously at a nail on her right hand. 'Yeah,' she replied quietly.

'Matty Hopkins' mobile phone is missing,' Nick stated, trying to make eye contact with her. 'We believe that it's here in your flat.'

'No.' Layla scowled and then shook her head adamantly. 'I don't know what you're talking about.'

'Okay.' Nick raised a doubtful brow. 'Well, our digital forensics team have triangulated the signal from Matty's phone and it's definitely here.'

Layla shrugged. 'I haven't seen it.'

Nick's instinct was that she was lying to him. 'Maybe Matty left it here by accident?'

'No... I don't know,' she said, starting to get flustered. 'I've just told you that I haven't seen it.'

'Right,' Nick said casually with a nod. 'I'm afraid we are going to have to search your flat and look for it. This is a murder investigation, so my team are going to be turning your flat upside down to find it.'

Layla's eyes widened anxiously.

Right, she is definitely lying to me, Nick thought.

'But if you do happen to know where it is,' he said in an even tone, 'then the best thing is for you to hand it over to me now. Before I call my search team in.'

There was an awkward silence.

Layla looked away awkwardly. 'Okay,' she whispered defensively.

'Can you show me where it is please, Layla?' he asked softly.

She got up and headed for a small table that had a lamp on it.

'If you can just show me,' Nick said as he pulled blue forensic gloves and an evidence bag from his pocket.

'It's just behind that lamp,' she explained sheepishly.

Moving the lamp to one side, Nick saw a black iPhone. He reached over, picked it up and put it into the clear evidence bag.

Layla went back to the chair and sat curled up and hugging her legs. She stared into space.

Sitting back down on the sofa, Nick removed his gloves and looked over at her. 'Can you tell me why you didn't tell anyone that Matty's phone was here?'

Layla shrugged defensively.

'Matty was murdered,' Nick said. 'But when my colleagues spoke to you yesterday, you didn't mention that you had his phone here. And that means that you were deliberately hiding evidence from our investigation. That's a criminal offence, Layla.' He waited for a beat as he watched her anxiety grow. 'So, can you tell me why you deliberately hid the fact that you had Matty's phone?'

Layla pursed her lips as her eyes filled with tears. She took a deep breath. 'There are photos and a video on there,' she sniffed. 'I didn't have his code so...'

'What are the photos and video of?' Nick asked, even though he could make an educated guess.

Layla shook her head. 'I don't want to say.'

'Are the photos and the video of you and Matthew having sex here on Saturday night?' Nick asked gently.

Layla looked down at the floor and nodded.

CHAPTER 31

Garrow and French were back at the holiday park. French had contacted Nick to inform him what they had seen on the CCTV at the petrol station. Although it was by no means incriminating, Miles Hopkins certainly needed to explain why he had filled up four cans of petrol only days before one of the cabins on his holiday park had been set alight… with petrol. Obviously Garrow couldn't think of a good reason why Hopkins would want to murder his own son, but as with all good police work, it was a matter of following the evidence and eliminating what they could from the investigation.

They headed towards the ivy-clad house where Miles and Jane Hopkins lived on site. At an educated guess, Garrow thought the house was probably late Victorian and so about one hundred years old. It had large windows that had Victorian Gothic peaks with white cast iron tracery. The flowerbeds in front of the house were populated by colourful wallflowers, daffodils and anemones.

They went through a small iron gate with a carved gate post and walked up the red tiled garden path that was dotted with clammy dark moss. Above the front door was an oval of stained glass. Garrow assumed that this was the original manor house for the surrounding land which now comprised the holiday park.

French gave an authoritative knock on the door and took a step back.

'Nice house,' Garrow remarked.

French pulled a face. 'If you like that sort of thing.'

'You don't I take it?'

'It's a bit twee for my liking,' French remarked under his breath.

The front door opened and Jane peered out. She looked tired and drawn.

'Yes?' she asked.

'We've got a couple of things we'd like to clarify with you and your husband, if that's okay?' French said.

Jane blinked, gave a slight nod and then opened the front door so that they could go in. 'Of course,' she said very quietly.

The hallway was wide and long. A huge ornate mirror dominated the wall inside.

'We can go in here,' she said, lost in thought.

They entered a large, airy living room which smelt of polish and old books. Most of the furniture was thick oak. The walls were dotted with tasteful black and white photographs and posters from art exhibitions.

'Please sit down,' Jane said.

French and Garrow sat on a low sofa where flattened embroidered cushions had been lined up to add a splash of colour to the deep chestnut leather.

'Sorry,' she said shaking her head. 'Would you like coffee or tea?'

'No, we're fine thank you,' French reassured her.

Jane sat forwards on an armchair in a huddled position. She looked over at them. 'Have you found... anyone?' she asked. Her voice was quiet.

'We are following several lines of enquiry at the moment,' French explained. 'And as soon as we have anything significant, we'll inform you straight away.'

Garrow's eyes had been drawn to some family photos that were in frames and sat on the top of an upright piano and a small table beside that. Several of the photos featured a young girl with long blonde hair in ringlets. Two of the images showed Miles, Jane and Matty Hopkins with the young girl. Garrow could only assume that this was their daughter, although no one had mentioned her.

Garrow made a subtle gesture towards the photos. 'I was just looking at your photographs,' he stated softly. 'Do you have a daughter?'

'Sophie?' Jane said with a sad smile. 'Yes. We did. But we lost her nearly four years ago.'

Garrow nodded empathetically. 'I'm so sorry to hear that.' Even though they were there to ask Hopkins about his visit to the garage, Garrow couldn't help but feel compassion for a couple who had lost two children.

French looked over at her. 'Actually it was your husband that we're particularly keen to talk to today.'

'He's not here,' Jane replied a little too quickly.

Garrow suspected that she was lying. Her face and body language betrayed her rather too easily.

There was noise from upstairs. It was the sound of someone walking around.

There was an awkward silence.

Jane did her best to ignore the sound.

French sat forwards. 'It really would be useful to talk to your husband,' he said softly, giving her the opportunity to move past her lie.

'Sorry,' she said awkwardly. 'I thought he was sleeping upstairs. We're both finding it difficult to get any sleep.'

French nodded. 'Of course. I understand.'

Jane gestured to the door. 'I'll go and see if he's up to coming down.'

'If you would, that would be great,' French reassured her.

She left the room.

French looked at Garrow and said under his breath, 'What do you think?'

Garrow ran a palm along his jaw, as if to aid his thinking. 'Seems strange that she lied about him being in the house.'

French shrugged. 'Maybe she was just being overprotective.'

Something had been weighing on Garrow's mind since their arrival. He needed to run it past French. 'Sarge, we have CCTV of Miles Hopkins buying cans of petrol three days ago. Eyewitnesses also claim that he was the first on scene. But this house is ten minutes from those cabins. How did he get there so quickly?'

French narrowed his eyes and thought for a moment. 'But why would he deliberately burn down a cabin and kill his own son?'

'What if he didn't?' Garrow suggested.

'What do you mean?'

'What if Hopkins didn't know Matty was inside that cabin? We know that Matty had been drinking heavily. And he's got the keys to Cabin 5. He knows that the cabin is vacant, so he decides to let himself in and sleep it off there.'

'I'm lost.' French paused in thought. 'Why is Miles Hopkins burning down a cabin deliberately?'

Garrow was about to answer, but before he had chance...

'Insurance?' French suggested.

'Maybe,' Garrow murmured. 'If you've got a cash flow crisis, you burn down a cabin and take the insurance. It's got to be worth looking at?'

'Yeah, it has,' French agreed.

Before they could continue, Jane and Hopkins walked into the room.

'I understand that you need to speak to me about something?' he said as he came and sat down.

'Yes, that's right,' French replied lightly. 'It's just routine but we have to look at everything in an investigation like this.'

'My wife tells me that you don't have a suspect at the moment,' Hopkins said with a frustrated sigh.

'As I explained to your wife, we are pursuing various lines of enquiry at the moment.'

Hopkins rolled his eyes. 'That sounds like police jargon for saying that you don't have any idea who did this to our son.'

Garrow could feel the tension build in the room. Confronting Hopkins with what they had discovered wasn't going to go well.

Taking his phone from his pocket, Garrow trawled through to find the photograph he'd taken at the petrol station. He leaned forwards to show Hopkins. 'If you could take a look at this for us please?' he said, preparing himself for an outburst of anger. If Hopkins really was guilty of pouring petrol on Cabin 5 and setting it alight, he would need to cover his guilt by appearing incensed by such speculation. If he wasn't guilty of starting the fire, he might still be outraged.

Hopkins took Garrow's phone and squinted at the screen. 'What exactly am I looking at?' he asked, sounding irritated.

French leaned forwards. 'This is taken from CCTV footage at the Old Colwyn Petrol Station. We believe that's you and your vehicle there on Thursday afternoon?'

Hopkins' face twisted in anger as he thrust the phone back into Garrow's hand. 'What the hell has that got to do with who killed my son?' he thundered.

'In an investigation like this,' Garrow said calmly, 'we really do have to explore every avenue.'

Hopkins' face was now red. 'And you think that because I filled up a couple of petrol cans at this petrol station, and burnt down that cabin with my son inside! This is outrageous.'

'Please calm down, Miles,' Jane said. 'These officers are only doing their job.'

Hopkins glared at her. 'They're wasting their bloody time looking at the CCTV at petrol stations when they should be out there looking for the person who killed our son!' He waved his finger towards Garrow's phone. 'If that's all you've got, then God help us.'

'This holiday park is nearly ninety acres in size,' Jane explained very calmly. 'You can imagine how much upkeep that takes. We have several ride-on mowers up here.' She looked at Hopkins. 'I assume my husband was getting petrol for them?'

Hopkins took a deep breath, then curled his finger and headed for the door. 'Come with me, please.'

Garrow exchanged a look with French.

They got up and followed Hopkins out of the living room and down the hallway to the front door.

Garrow had no idea why Hopkins had asked them to follow him, but it seemed prudent to do so.

They walked across the well-tended lawn trying to keep up with Hopkins who was about ten yards ahead of them.

They approached a very large wooden shed with an asphalt roof. Reaching into his pocket, Hopkins pulled out a bunch of keys. He unlocked the door and then looked back at them.

'Well, come on then,' he barked.

The shed was full of equipment – spades, rakes, ladders etc. It smelled of damp and grass cuttings.

On the far side, there were three red ride-on Mountfield mowers.

Hopkins marched towards them like a man possessed. Then he pointed down at the ground where the petrol cans were sitting. He picked one up and held it up high. 'Do you want to check them to see if they have petrol in them?'

'That won't be necessary,' French replied calmly.

'No, I didn't think so,' Hopkins snapped as he put the petrol can down. 'Why don't you get on and do your job properly,' he snarled as he marched past them and out of the shed.

Garrow spotted that Jane was standing in the doorway. She was looking upset and deep in thought as they came over.

'I would really like to have my son's mobile phone back as soon as possible,' she said quietly. 'There are some family photographs on there and I don't want to lose them.'

Garrow noticed that her eyes were glassy and a tear ran down her face.

'Of course,' French reassured her.

The mention of Matty's mobile phone sparked a thought. 'Does the name Layla Hughes mean anything to you?' Garrow asked.

Garrow wasn't about to reveal that she had been the person they'd found in possession of Matty's phone.

'Layla?' She clearly did know her.

'You know her?' French asked to clarify.

'Yes, of course. She used to work here at the park.'

'But not anymore?' Garrow asked.

'No,' she said and cleared her throat, 'we had to let her go.'

'Can you tell us why?'

'There was an altercation with one of her co-workers,' she explained.

'Was it serious?' French asked.

Jane shrugged but it felt as if there was something more to it. 'We took care of it internally.'

Garrow raised his brows. 'Can you tell us what the altercation was about?'

She shook her head. 'No idea. But Layla's behaviour was violent and unacceptable. There was no way we could allow her to work here again.'

'Did you call the police?' French enquired.

'No.'

'Did you sack the co-worker too?'

'No,' Jane replied. 'There was no need. She was an innocent party in the incident.'

French frowned. 'And you have no idea why Layla acted in that way towards this person?'

'No.'

Garrow looked at her. 'Could you give us her name?'

'Zoe Solomon.'

CHAPTER 32

Clapham Common

April 1997

Ruth pushed Ella in her pushchair up to the top of Balham Hill, across the road by Clapham Common tube station, and then through the common itself towards the swings and playground. She was so indignant, so full of rage, that she hadn't noticed any of her surroundings for over twenty minutes.

Her feckless, useless partner, Dan, had just walked out on her and Ella. *The utter fucking cheek of it!* She was furious with him, but she was also furious with herself.

It had been forty-eight hours since she'd discovered a woman's name and phone number scrawled on a scrap of paper in the back pocket of his jeans. She also knew that he'd lied about DJ'ing in a pub in Hammersmith two nights ago. And rather than throw him out of the flat they shared in Balham, she'd allowed him to leave her.

I'm such an idiot!

She couldn't believe that she had allowed herself to become a single mum. It's just not how she saw her life panning out. However, once she got past the hurt pride, Ruth knew that in the long run she would prefer life without him. She didn't trust him for starters. He seemed to only take care of Ella when it was convenient for him – which was rarely. And even though he was about to turn thirty, he acted as if he was a twenty-year-old single man-child.

The worst part of it was that Ruth had allowed him to get away with it for far too long. For some reason, she had ignored the lies, the unexplained phone numbers, that he rarely wanted sex with her anymore and that he drank and smoked weed like an entitled student. In fact, she had reached the point where everything about him either irritated her or made her want to do him physical harm.

So, why hadn't she confronted him and thrown him out? What was she afraid of? Of being alone… or of being judged for having a failed relationship and being a single mum? She could sense there was something holding her back. No one would have blamed her for kicking him out. Everyone had told her that Dan was a waste of space for years. He earned a pittance working as an occasional roadie and DJ. She had pleaded for him to get *a proper job* so they didn't have to worry about how they were going to pay the rent, bills and childcare. But Dan lived in his own little world where he still believed that when he got his big break, he would be flown out to Ibiza to DJ and earn a fortune. But often her anger had turned to pity.

As Ruth and Ella reached the swings in the middle of Clapham Common, close to the pond, Ruth's head was spinning. She unclipped Ella from her pushchair and took off her thick zebra-striped blanket. Holding her hand, they went over to the swings. She lifted Ella up and placed her into the swing that had a safety bar.

'Push me! Push me, Mummy!' Ella yelled.

'Okay, okay, give me a chance,' Ruth laughed as she went around the back and gave the swing a gentle push.

Across the road, the old letting agent office had been taken over by a flash new estate agents and the convenience store was now a smart bar on two floors. South London was changing before Ruth's eyes. Gentrification had arrived, and it looked like Balham was going the same way as Clapham had gone in the last eighteen months. The working-class families from SW4 and SW12 were migrating to places like Crystal Palace and Peckham, where housing was much cheaper. Her grandparents wouldn't recognise some parts of south-west London now.

Ruth felt something in her coat pocket. As she reached inside, she pulled out her camera. She had no idea why it was in there, but she thought she might as well take a photo of Ella.

Waving the camera, Ruth marched around the front of the swing. 'I'm just going to take a photo of you.' Ruth pointed the camera at Ella and said, 'Say cheese!'

'Cheeeeeeeese!' Ella shouted with a huge grin as she rocked herself in the swing.

Ruth went over to Ella's side. She wasn't going to allow Dan to spoil everything.

Fuck him. We're better off without him, she thought resiliently.

Crouching down, she turned the camera around as she tried to take a photo of both her and Ella. She had no idea if it would work.

'Would you like me to take a photo of the both of you?' said a voice.

It was a woman in her sixties, who was pushing what appeared to be her grandson in another swing. She gave Ruth and Ella a kind smile.

'Oh, yes please,' Ruth said as she walked over and handed her the camera. 'Thank you.'

The woman pointed the camera at them. 'Okay, ready?'

'Yes,' Ella yelled.

'Three, two, one, go,' the woman said with a laugh as she took the photo and then handed the camera back to Ruth.

Taking a deep breath, Ruth realised that when she woke up in the morning it would be a whole new chapter in her life. She was determined that it was going to be a stable and loving one. For Ella's sake.

CHAPTER 33

Nick had made the short journey from Colwyn Bay up to the holiday park. Despite the SOCOs having searched Matthew Hopkins' static caravan, Nick had decided to have another look himself. It wasn't that he didn't trust the SOCOs to do a thorough job. It was more that he wanted to get a deeper sense of what Matthew had been like as a person. Were there any clues in the caravan that weren't immediately obvious to a forensics team?

As he made his way down through the row of static caravans, his presence was clocked by various holiday-makers. Wearing a dark suit and a black raincoat, he guessed that it was fairly obvious that he was a copper.

The small wooden staircase and door to Matty's caravan had blue and white police evidence tape strung across them. Moving the tape up, Nick ducked underneath, pulled on his blue forensic gloves and went inside. The small living area was very clean and tidy. It was dominated by an L-shaped sofa made from a grey material. Two blue cushions with white anchors had been placed at either end. The floors were constructed from a light-coloured wood. The kitchen area was small with an electric hob and oven. A tea towel with the same anchor pattern hung from the oven handle.

Nick began to open the cupboards. There was nothing remarkable inside. Beans, soup, pasta and noodles. There were some photographs attached to a nearby fridge. Most of them showed Matty partying either in the park or on holiday. There weren't any family photographs, which Nick thought was a little strange.

Nick went through to the bedroom where he found a double bed, a wrought iron headboard and a light blue duvet. Shoes and trainers had been positioned in a neat row. Opening the small wardrobe, he saw a few shirts and jackets on hangers. He squatted down and searched the base of the wardrobe. In his experience, this was a place where people tended to hide anything they didn't want anyone to find. Over the years he'd found everything from firearms and drugs to kinky sex toys and pornographic magazines and films. However, apart from an empty gym bag and a pair of muddy walking boots, there was nothing.

Nick stood up, took a step back and knocked a bedside table with his thigh. The bedside light that was on it tumbled to the floor.

'Shit!' He said under this breath.

As he picked it up, he saw that something was stuck with tape into a small cavity on the base of the light. Reaching in, Nick pulled it out.

It was a computer memory stick.

Whatever was on there, it was clearly something Matthew had been keen to hide. Despite his confidence in the SOCO's initial search, Nick was annoyed that this had been missed. He would need to take it up with the chief forensic officer at Llancastell nick in the next few days.

Nick took out a small, clear plastic evidence bag from his pocket and placed the memory stick inside. He would get the digital forensic guys to have a look at it.

As he took a step outside the bedroom into the narrow hallway, he heard a noise coming from the door. It sounded like someone was coming in.

Nick froze. The caravan was still officially a crime scene and there were clear signs and tape outside to make sure no one came in.

Who the hell is that?

He saw a figure come inside.

It was Jane Hopkins.

She saw him and jumped out of her skin. 'Jesus! You scared me!'

'Sorry,' Nick said, one eyebrow raised quizzically.

'I'm probably not supposed to be in here…' she said, looking a little lost.

'Not really,' Nick replied, but he gave her an empathetic look. She had lost her son and maybe she just wanted to be in the place where he had lived.

She spotted that he was wearing forensic gloves. 'Did you find anything?'

Nick shook his head. 'I'm afraid not.' He wasn't about to tell her that he'd found a hidden memory stick.

Jane gestured back to the door. 'I should probably go then.'

'Actually, I came here because I wanted to get a sense of what Matthew was like,' he admitted.

'How do you mean?' Jane asked.

'I know this is incredibly hard for you and your husband,' Nick said softly, 'but I need to know why someone would want to harm Matty.'

Jane took a deep breath and didn't say anything for a few seconds. Then she slowly shook her head. 'I just don't know. He was a lovely young man. Very funny, so full of life. He really lived his life to the full…' Then her eyes filled with tears. 'Sorry, I…'

'There's no need to apologise,' Nick reassured her. 'And he never fell out with anyone? No arguments? He didn't upset anybody recently?'

Jane's eyes moved in a way that indicated that she had just thought of something.

'I get the feeling there is something?' Nick said gently, trying to encourage her to be honest.

'He was my son…' Jane sniffed as she wiped her face. Then she shrugged. 'But he… how shall I put it… had an eye for the ladies. He was a young man in his twenties. He was sewing his wild oats, you know?' Then Jane gave Nick a meaningful look. 'But I'm not sure how respectful he was when it came to their feelings. You know, boys will be boys. I think he'd upset his fair share of girls around here, but I'm pretty sure that none of them would do anything like this.'

Nick wondered if Matty's poor treatment of women was the key to his death.

CHAPTER 34

It was now dark outside as Sarah sat beside Ruth in the ICU. Ella, who had been home to shower and grab a couple of hours' sleep, sat looking at her phone. The rhythmic noise of the ventilator had become an integral part of the audio tapestry of the room. Sarah watched Ruth's chest as it went up and down in a gentle tempo. Then she looked at Ruth's face which was partially obscured by the ventilator that had been taped to her mouth.

What's she going to be like when she comes round? Sarah wondered uneasily. Were they going to get the same Ruth back? What if her speech or mobility had been affected by the cardiac arrest? It was easy to tell herself that they would just deal with all that and just getting Ruth back alive would be enough. But there was a nagging hope and desire to get the person she'd fallen in love with back. What if Ruth's personality had completely changed? She'd heard of people who had suffered brain damage and came out of a coma with completely unrecognisable character changes.

Ella smiled and then turned her phone to show Sarah. 'This popped up on my Facebook timeline. It's a photo from ten years ago.'

Sarah leaned forwards and squinted to have a look. The photo was of Ella in her mid-teens, wearing a *One*

Direction T-shirt and standing with her arm around Sarah. They were both grinning.

'Bloody hell, *One Direction*,' Sarah said, shaking her head. 'I don't think I heard any of the first few songs because of all the screaming.'

'Hammersmith Apollo,' Ella said, looking at the photo. 'Mum said it was just like being at a Wham! concert she'd been to twenty years earlier.'

The door to the room entered and the young doctor with glasses came in.

His entrance startled Sarah every time as she watched his face intently for good news, bad news or no news. His expression seemed to be the same when delivering any of those.

He went over to check on Ruth for a few moments. Sometimes he did this and then just left. This time he turned to look at them.

'The latest CAT scan reveals that the swelling around Ruth's brain has reduced to a very low level. And that's a very good sign,' he explained.

'What happens now?' Sarah asked anxiously.

'We will no longer administer any more anaesthetics,' he stated, 'and so Ruth will slowly come out of her coma.'

Ella's eyes searched his face. 'How long will that take?'

'Hard to tell. Could be as long as twelve hours. But it could be two to three hours.' Then he gave them a serious look. 'Ruth will be both confused and agitated when she starts to regain consciousness. And, as I've explained, we have no way of knowing the damage that the cardiac arrest may have caused to her brain. So you have to prepare yourselves for that and be as patient as you can be.'

Sarah felt her stomach tighten as she took in his words.

CHAPTER 35

'Right guys, if I can have your attention,' Nick said as he strode across the CID office, heading for the scene board. However, before he could start, his eye was drawn to a figure coming through the double doors.

It was Georgie.

She gave everyone a cheeky grin. 'Sorry I'm late, boss. Some twat parked in my usual spot.'

Everyone laughed, clapped and generally welcomed her back.

Nick's eyes crinkled with good humour. 'I thought you were going to stay at home for at least a couple of days?'

Georgie strode over to her desk, pulled out her chair and plonked herself down. 'What, and miss all the action?' she joked. Then she took out a pad of paper and a pen before pointing over to the scene board. 'This is that fire at the holiday park in Colwyn Bay?'

Nick knew that Georgie should be at home convalescing. But she was here now, and maybe keeping busy at work really was better for her than sitting at home. He nodded. 'Erm, yes. Correct.'

Georgie sat back. 'Right, well you guys get me up to speed. I'm more than capable of chasing leads and making phone calls.' She gave Nick a knowing smile. 'If that's all right?'

Nick shook his head. He had to give it to her. She had what was once described in a film he'd seen as *gumption*. In the old days, he might have said that she *had balls*, but he assumed that that was no longer appropriate these days.

'That's more than all right, Georgie,' he laughed. 'It's good to have you back.' He turned back to the scene board. 'Right, where were we?' He then pointed to a photo. 'Miles Hopkins? What have we got?'

French looked over. 'We have the CCTV of Hopkins buying four cans of petrol last Thursday. When confronted, he showed us the cans and claimed they were for some of the ride-on mowers they use on site.'

'Seems reasonable,' Nick suggested, unconvinced that Hopkins could be a suspect for the murder of his own son.

French continued. 'Actually, Jim has a theory that I think is worth looking at.'

'Go for it,' Nick said.

'I did a search at Companies House,' Garrow began. 'The Pen-y-Bryn Holiday Park made a loss of £850,000 last tax year. Their application for a swimming pool and leisure complex was withdrawn last year due to lack of finance.' He pointed to his computer screen. 'Each of those luxury cabins is insured for £150,000 to fully replace. If the holiday park was on the verge of bankruptcy, maybe Miles Hopkins planned to burn one of the cabins down to release some capital? There is no reason that he would know that his son had gone in there. It's just a tragic accident.'

French nodded in agreement. 'Boss, Jim and I timed the walk from the Hopkins' home over to Cabin 5. It's around twelve minutes.' He looked down at his notes. 'But according to the emergency call records, the 999 call was made at 11:55 p.m. and then a call was made to Hopkins directly after that. But eyewitnesses put him at the scene of the fire at midnight. How did he get over there in under five minutes?'

'It's not going to be enough to get a search warrant unfortunately. And it doesn't explain why the key was found in the lock on the outside. If Hopkins thought the cabin was empty, why would he need to bring a key with him to lock the door from outside? That doesn't make sense,' Nick said in frustration as he thought out loud. 'I'm not ruling that hypothesis out, Jim, but that doesn't add up.' Then Nick gestured to two other photos. 'What about Kevin Ball and Kat Mount?'

'We know Ball lied about returning to the caravan to get a bottle of vodka because the door was locked,' French said. 'Layla Hughes claimed that Matty left her flat after they'd had sex and was going to buy cocaine from Kat. However, Kat told us that Matty never arrived, which we know is true from the toxicology report. But we also don't have any motive at the moment for either of them to murder Matty.'

'What about the altercation between Ball and Matty that Miles Hopkins told us about?' Garrow said.

French shrugged. 'Maybe it was what Ball told us. Matty throwing his weight around as the boss's son and having a pop at Ball about his timekeeping.'

'Okay,' Nick said. 'And Kat Mount is currently on bail for possession and intent to supply Class A drugs?'

'Yes,' Garrow confirmed.

'Then we come to Layla Hughes,' Nick said, tapping his forefinger against her photograph. 'We know that she and Matty had sex at her flat at around eleven p.m. She claims that he left there and headed back to the holiday park. Matty left his mobile phone there. Layla says that he had taken a video of them having sex which is why she didn't hand the phone over. That phone is currently with the digital forensics team along with a memory stick that I found hidden in Matty's caravan.' Nick then rubbed his beard for a second.

Garrow checked his notes and announced, 'Layla was sacked from the holiday park after a violent altercation with another girl, Zoe Solomon. Jane Hopkins didn't know what the altercation was about, but it sounded serious.'

Nick nodded. 'Okay. Jim and Dan, let's see what Zoe Solomon can tell us about what happened between her and Layla. Do we have the CCTV from the holiday park yet?'

Garrow pointed. 'It's just come through.'

'And let's have a look at Matty's phone and bank records, plus his social media,' Nick said. 'Back here at five p.m. for a catch up please.'

CHAPTER 36

Half an hour later French and Garrow walked across the holiday park towards the static caravan where they had been told Zoe Solomon lived. The wind was whipping up an eerie melody as they approached. Gulls cawed above their heads as they ducked and swooped on the air currents.

Unlike some of the scruffier caravans, Zoe Solomon's caravan looked well kept. There were potted plants along the decking at one end with a small table and wrought iron chairs.

French went to the door and gave it a knock.

A few seconds later a young woman in her early twenties peered out. She was Afro-Caribbean with braided hair and bright, kind eyes.

French and Garrow showed her their warrant cards. 'DS French and DC Garrow, Llancastell CID. We're looking for Zoe Solomon?'

'Yes,' Zoe said with a nervous blink.

'We'd like to ask you a couple of routine questions,' French explained. 'If we can come in, it won't take more than a few minutes.'

'Erm, yes, of course,' Zoe replied hesitantly as she opened the door to let them inside.

The interior of the caravan was immaculate and taste-fully decorated with shades of warm orange and dark red.

Zoe gestured to the L-shaped sofa that was in her living area. 'Would you like to sit down?' she asked quietly.

'Thank you,' Garrow replied, giving her a kind smile.

Zoe sat down on the armchair looking anxious. 'Sorry, would you like some tea?'

French smiled. 'Thank you, but we're fine.'

Garrow took out his notepad and pen. 'You work here at the park, is that right, Zoe?'

'Yes, that's right,' she replied with a nervous smile.

'What do you do?' French asked.

'Cleaning mainly. Laundry,' she said. 'Sometimes I help out at the kids' club in the summer.'

'How long have you been working here?' Garrow enquired.

Zoe took a moment and then said, 'Nearly two years.'

French leaned forwards. 'Did you know Matty Hopkins?'

Zoe took a visible breath and nodded sadly.

Garrow stopped writing and asked, 'Did you know him well?'

'I guess,' she said, but her manner had become uncomfortable. 'Matty has been working here the whole time that I've been here. And we all know each other. We hung out sometimes.'

Garrow turned a page of his notepad. 'We understand that you had some kind of altercation with Layla Hughes a few months ago?'

Zoe narrowed her eyes. 'Altercation?' She seemed to have taken offence to the wording of the question.

'Jane Hopkins told us that there was some kind of row?' French stated.

'It wasn't a row,' she said indignantly. 'She bloody attacked me.' She pointed to her mouth. 'She punched me right in the face and cut my lip. Psycho.'

'Right,' French said. 'But you didn't call the police?'

'Jane asked me not to call them. She said that Layla had been sacked and there was no need to get the police involved.'

'Do you know why Layla attacked you?'

Zoe didn't answer for a few seconds. The question had made her uneasy and she visibly took a breath.

'Zoe?' French asked, encouraging her to give an answer.

'It's not something that I really want to talk about,' she muttered under her breath. Whatever it was, she clearly felt it was embarrassing.

French said quietly, 'Zoe, this is a murder investigation. It's very important that you answer all our questions fully so we can find out what happened to Matty and why. Do you understand that?'

She nodded and then blurted out, 'She attacked me because of Matty.'

'I don't understand.' French furrowed his brow. 'Why would Layla attack you because of Matty?'

'She said I'd slept with him.'

Garrow sat forwards with a quizzical expression. 'Did you sleep with him?'

'Yes,' she said quietly.

'Were Layla and Matty in a relationship when you slept with him?' French said.

'Only in her head,' Zoe snorted.

'Why do you say that?'

'Matty was a player,' she said, shaking her head. 'I think he'd slept with most of the girls at one time or another.

But he never had a girlfriend. Layla seemed to get it into her head that she and Matty were together. And when it got out that me and him had spent the night together, she went totally mental. That's when she attacked me.'

'But they weren't together?' Garrow asked to clarify.

'God no,' she said emphatically. 'He told me he thought Layla was a bit of a psycho.'

'And how did he react to Layla attacking you?' French said.

Zoe gave a wry laugh. 'He just loved it. Girls fighting over him. I don't know what it was, but he had this ability to charm almost anyone into bed. Most of us thought it was a bit of a laugh. He's a good-looking bloke.' Then Zoe caught herself. 'I mean, he was… But Layla isn't right up there,' she said, pointing to her head. 'She said if I went near Matty again, she'd kill me.'

CHAPTER 37

Ruth became aware of noises around her. Someone was talking but the words sounded muffled and incomprehensible. As she swallowed, she got an excruciating pain in the back of her throat. It felt like someone had cut it with a razor blade. Her head throbbed and felt like it was gripped in a vice.

She began to feel the weight of sheets and a blanket on top of her. An electronic sound beeped in a constant rhythm. Moving her fingers, she could feel the material of the blanket with the tip of her forefinger.

The voices seemed to get a little louder. Her instant reaction was to become very irritable at their tone and volume.

Shut up. Stop talking, she snapped inside her head. She just wanted peace and quiet.

As she began to rouse, the muscles around her right eye and cheek began to twitch. The thought of trying to open her eyelids felt insurmountable. It was as if they were made from lead.

Here we go, she thought as she put every ounce of effort into prising them open.

The daylight was stark and it made her squint and close her eyes again.

'Ruth?' said a woman's voice.

Who is that?

Taking a deep breath, Ruth felt a sharp pain down in her abdomen.

Wow, that hurts! Where the hell am I?

She opened her eyes very slowly again.

At first, all she could see were two blurred faces looking down at her.

Then they came into focus.

The woman smiled at her. 'Ruth, you're in hospital but you're okay,' she reassured her.

Ruth looked around and could see she was lying in a bed in a single room somewhere in a hospital.

She frowned and tried to speak. 'Where…' The words seemed to stick inside her throat somewhere. It was agonising.

'It's okay, Mum. Don't try and speak,' another voice said. Looking to her left, she saw someone grab a jug of water, pour some into a plastic beaker and bring it over to her. 'Here you go. Just sip on this very slowly.'

Ruth still couldn't focus her eyes fully, but she felt the beaker against her lips and the coldness of the water. She took a sip, but as soon as it trickled down the back of her throat it stung. She coughed and tried to sit up.

'Take it easy.'

They helped her move, and adjusted a pillow so that her head was elevated a little.

Her vision now cleared.

On her right, an attractive woman in her forties gave her a kind smile. 'There you go.'

On her left, a young woman in her twenties came and took her hand. 'Hey, Mum. Don't worry. It's going to be okay.'

Ruth was so confused and started to feel very anxious.

'Who... who are you?' she croaked as she frowned at the young woman. It seemed so weird that this person was calling her Mum and holding her hand.

'It's Ella, your daughter,' the other woman said as if she was mad. 'I'm Sarah.'

Ruth felt a surge of panic overwhelm her. 'But... I don't know who you are.'

CHAPTER 38

Nick tapped at the keys on the computer in the DI's office. If anything, the mounds of paperwork around him had multiplied. He loosened his tie and undid the top button of his shirt.

His mobile phone rang. It was Sarah. He instantly felt his stomach churn.

'Sarah?' he said, answering the phone.

'Hey, Nick,' Sarah said quietly.

In that second, he tried to analyse the tone of her voice. Was this going to be terrible news?

Before he could reach any conclusion, Sarah said, 'Ruth's regained consciousness.'

'That's great,' Nick said, but his relief was tempered by Sarah's cautious tone. 'Isn't it?'

'Erm… it is,' Sarah said, but her voice trembled as if she were holding back tears.

Nick felt very uneasy. 'What's wrong, Sarah?'

'She doesn't recognise us,' Sarah said, and then it was all too much for her and he could hear her start to cry. 'And her speech is very slurred.'

'Right,' Nick said, trying to remain calm. 'What have the doctors said?'

'They've said it's going to take time. But seeing her like that…' Sarah sobbed. 'She just looked so confused and so scared. It was horrible, Nick.'

'Of course it was. But she's been in a coma. It's going to take time for her to recover from that.' Nick was trying to reassure her, but inside he was scared that Ruth just wasn't going to recover fully. 'I'll try and come over as soon as I can.'

'It's fine. She's so exhausted that she's in and out of sleep most of the time.'

'Okay, but I'll come over later.'

'Thank you, Nick.'

Nick ended the call and took a few moments to compose himself. As he went out into the CID office, he spotted Georgie looking intently at her computer screen.

'You okay?' he asked as he approached.

'Yeah, all good,' she replied, and then gave him a quizzical look. 'Anything from the hospital?'

'Yes… Ruth has regained consciousness and is now out of the induced coma.'

'Is she okay?'

'Yeah, she's fine,' he lied. He didn't want to worry Georgie unnecessarily, she'd been through enough in recent days. 'Sarah said she's just sleeping.'

'Can we go and see her?'

'Sarah said she'd let us know when Ruth's up to visitors.'

'Of course,' Georgie said, and then gave a half smile. 'But that's good news isn't it?'

'Yes, it is,' Nick said, but he was still incredibly concerned by what Sarah had actually told him. However, he needed to keep busy and distract himself. He pointed to Georgie's computer. 'What have you got?'

'Digital forensics have pulled all the text messages from Matthew Hopkins' phone. We have a series of messages from Layla Hughes in the days leading up to the murder.

Isn't she the woman who slept with him the night he died?'

'Yes, that's right. What are the messages about?'

Georgie gave him a dark look. 'They're pretty disturbing.' She pointed to the screen. 'Read this one from the Thursday night.'

Nick leaned over and peered at the screen:

Matty:
Were you actually standing outside my caravan just now? WTF!

Layla:
No! It wasn't me.

Matty:
It was you. I know it was you. I took a fucking photo.

Layla:
It wasn't me, lol.

Matty:
You need help, Layla. I literally saw you.

Layla:
I just wanted to see you.

Matty:

I told you not to come near me. You're a
fucking psycho, Layla!

Layla:

Why are you so cold, Matty?

Matty:

If you come down here again, I'll call the
police. Understand?

Layla:

I just wanted to talk to you. That's all.

Matty:

Nothing to say to you.

Nick folded his arms across his chest. 'Doesn't sound good.'

Georgie appeared thoughtful. 'So, what were they doing sleeping together two nights later?' she asked to herself more than to Nick.

'Maybe Matty came on to her. He'd had a few drinks,' he suggested.

'What if Layla spiked his drink while they were in the flat? She thinks that if she drugs him, he won't be able to have sex with her and then just leave.'

'Maybe,' Nick said, thinking that Georgie's theory was definitely plausible. 'But Matty leaves anyway. She follows him back to the park, sees him go into Cabin 5 where he passes out because she's drugged him. Then she decides that if she can't have him, no one else can and she torches the place?'

'It's definitely possible,' Georgie agreed. She then clicked the computer, and a photo came up on the screen. 'I think this is the photo that Matty was talking about.'

Nick could see a slightly blurred photo that had been taken from inside the caravan. There was definitely a figure standing outside. They were wearing a dark baseball cap and a hoodie.

'Can you zoom in on that a bit?'

'I'll give it a go,' Georgie said as she clicked on the zoom function.

Nick looked again. Even though the image was slightly pixelated, he could see that it was definitely Layla Hughes standing there. There was something very creepy about the photograph and the expression on her face.

'Yeah, that's definitely her,' he said under his breath, starting to think that Layla was fast becoming their prime suspect. Then he had a thought. 'Can you do a quick property check for me?'

'Go for it,' Georgie said. 'What is it?'

'I think I remember that there's a flat above Layla Hughes' at *The Bay Café*. Can you do a search and find out if there is, and who owns it?'

'Right on it, boss,' Georgie said with a smile as she began to tap away at her computer.

Nick's phone rang again. It was French.

'Dan? How did it go with Zoe Solomon?' Nick asked.

'She claims that Layla Hughes attacked her and punched her in the face.'

'Did she say why?'

'Zoe had slept with Matty Hopkins,' French explained. 'Layla seemed to think that she and Matty were in some kind of relationship. So, she attacked Zoe and told her if she ever went near Matty again, she'd kill her. Zoe was insistent that Matty didn't have relationships with anyone and it was all in Layla's head. She described Layla as a psycho.'

'Okay. That's starting to fit the picture we're getting of her here,' Nick admitted.

Georgie gestured to her computer screen. 'You were right. There is another flat above *The Bay Café*. It's owned by a Margaret Roseblade.'

'I need you to go back to Colwyn Bay,' Nick said to French in an urgent tone. 'There's a flat above Layla Hughes' that belongs to a Margaret Roseblade. See if she heard or saw anything on Saturday night.'

'We're on it, boss,' French said.

CHAPTER 39

French and Garrow sped out of the holiday park and headed for Colwyn Bay. There were banks of dark green trees that lined the side of the main coastal road. However, wherever the trees parted, Garrow could see the Irish Sea stretching out to their right all the way to the horizon. As they reached a large brown sign that read *Bae Colwyn – Colwyn Bay*, there was also a sign to *Sŵ Fynydd Gymreig – Welsh Mountain Zoo*.

'Never been to the Welsh Mountain Zoo,' French stated as they rounded the bend. The trees completely disappeared and the vastness of the sea swept out before them. In the distance, the headland near Llandudno where the Great Orme was located jutted out into the sea.

'I don't believe in zoos,' Garrow said. It was something he felt strongly about.

'Of course you don't,' French said dryly.

'Seriously. What are Asian tigers doing roaming around an enclosure in North Wales?'

'I thought modern zoos were all conservation and animal friendly?' French said.

'Animal friendly?' Garrow snorted. 'Have you seen the elephant enclosure at Chester Zoo? Instead of being able to roam around their natural habitat of India, they're stuck in a dusty enclosure with a pond while dozens of school kids take photos. How is that *animal friendly*?'

French shrugged. 'Now that you've put it like that, I can see your point. I've never been a fan of zoos either.'

Garrow nodded. It was rare for him and French to agree on anything like that.

A few seconds later, they arrived at the sea front where *The Bay Café* was located and parked up.

Getting out of the car, Garrow glanced across the beach. The sunlight danced on the sea as small fishing boats bobbed on the waves and the salt-tinged wind blew against his cheeks.

They strode across the road and arrived at the front door to the side of *The Bay Café*. There were two buzzers – *Flat 1a* and *Flat 1b*. Layla Hughes' flat was *1a*.

French reached forwards and rang the buzzer for *Flat 1b*. If Layla Hughes and Matty Hopkins had rowed on Saturday night, then they wanted to know if the neighbour had heard or seen anything unusual in the time leading up to when Matty had left.

After a few seconds, French pushed the buzzer again.

They waited for a little longer.

Then there was the sound of someone approaching the door.

A woman in her forties looked out. She was large, with long dyed jet-black hair tied back with a patterned scarf. Her face was a delicate oval shape framed by sharp, dark eyebrows. She was wearing a long flowing kimono with a turquoise pattern, and she reminded Garrow of Mama Cass from the sixties hippy band *The Mamas & The Papas*.

'Can I help?' she asked. She had a London accent.

French got out his warrant card. 'DS French and DC Garrow. We're looking for a Margaret Roseblade?'

'Mags,' she corrected them casually. 'But yeah, that's me.'

'Okay if we come in for a minute?' French asked. 'It's just a couple of routine questions.'

Mags shrugged. 'Yeah, of course.'

They followed her up the stairs, past the entrance to Layla Hughes' flat and up to the top floor where they entered Mags' flat.

It was a little cluttered and untidy and smelled of spicy food and stale cigarettes.

She showed them into her living room and gestured to a sofa that was covered in a colourful crocheted blanket. The room was messy. There were piles of books on the floor, a stack of vinyl records, a lava lamp, a couple of Buddha heads and a large, framed photograph of a bearded George Harrison during *The Beatles' Sergeant Pepper's* era.

Garrow looked up at the photo. He'd always preferred George Harrison to Lennon or McCartney.

'George loved North Wales,' Mags said, pointing over at the photograph. 'Him and Paul played in a pub in Harlech in the late fifties. And George loved Portmeirion. He used to visit Brian Epstein there during the sixties. He even had his fiftieth birthday party there in 1993.'

Garrow nodded politely but he already knew most of that. He pulled out his notepad and pen.

'There are just a couple of questions we'd like to ask you regarding last Saturday night,' French explained.

'Oh, that's the night all that happened up at the holiday park, isn't it? It was in the papers,' Mags said, shaking her head. 'Terrible. Matty Hopkins? That was his name wasn't it?'

Garrow looked over at her. 'Did you know Matty?'

'Not really. I met him a few months ago, but we only spoke for a minute or two. Horrible, isn't it?'

'Yes… Can you tell us where you were last Saturday night?' French asked.

'Here all night,' she replied with a wry smile. 'I have a pretty boring life these days, I'm afraid.'

French gestured to the floor. 'And your neighbour downstairs is Layla Hughes?'

'That's right,' Mags replied.

'Do you have much to do with her?' he asked.

Mags thought carefully about her answer. 'Not if I can help it.'

Garrow looked up from his notepad. 'You don't get on?'

'She's not, as my dad used to say, quite the full shilling,' she said, pointing to the side of her head.

French leaned forwards. 'I'm not sure what you mean.'

Garrow knew that they were both aware of what she was implying but they wanted something more concrete.

'Layla can be a nasty piece of work. When she first moved in we got on really well. She'd pop up here for a cuppa or a drink and we'd put the world to rights. I thought she was a cracking girl.'

'What happened?' Garrow asked.

'A couple of months ago, I was putting my bins out,' Mags said. 'And that Matty was doing the same. I mean, he was putting out Layla's bins. And we got to chatting. Just a couple of minutes. Nothing much. Just passing the time of day really. Next day, she came up here like a banshee. She was asking me what I was talking to Matty about. She told me never to talk to him again. She was definitely not right in the head.'

Garrow exchanged a look with French. This was the picture they were getting of Layla Hughes from everyone they spoke to.

'And after that?' Garrow asked.

'Nothing. She's cut me dead. Now she walks straight past me in the street,' Mags said with raised eyebrows. 'Couple of days ago I went into the café to get a takeaway coffee. I saw her go over to another waitress to make sure she didn't have to serve me.' She shook her head. 'Jesus. I think all me and Matty talked about was the bloody weather.'

'And Saturday night?' French said. 'Did you see or hear anything suspicious?'

Mags pointed to the floor. 'I knew he was down there. I heard them at it, you know?'

'You heard them having sex?' Garrow asked to clarify.

'Yeah,' Mags replied. 'Something must have happened because I hadn't seen or heard him around for a couple of weeks. And then bloody World War Three broke out.'

French furrowed his brow. 'They were arguing?'

'Oh yeah,' Mags said. 'They were always bloody arguing. Shagging or arguing, that's all they seemed to do.'

'And you're sure it was Matty Hopkins in the flat downstairs?' Garrow enquired.

'Oh yeah,' Mags nodded. 'I'm not usually a busybody. But I heard the door downstairs slam. And I thought thank God for that.' She pointed to a window. 'So, I went and had a look outside. And I saw Matty heading off up the road.'

'Was he heading in the direction of the Pen-y-Bryn Holiday Park?'

'Yeah. I guessed he was going to cut through the woods,' Mags replied. 'Mind you, he was a bit worse for wear.'

Garrow looked up. 'He was drunk?'

'He was hammered,' Mags said, her eyes widening. 'Zig-zagging all over the bloody place.' Then she gave them both a quizzical look. 'You don't think Layla had something to do with what happened to Matty, do you?'

'It's something we can't discuss during an ongoing investigation,' French said dismissively.

Something about the question puzzled Garrow. 'Why would you think Layla could be involved in Matty's murder if you watched him walk off from here on his own?'

'Because she followed him.'

Garrow looked over at French. This was a significant piece of evidence. Up until now, they had assumed that Layla Hughes had told the truth – she had stayed in her flat once Matty had left.

'She followed him?' French asked.

'Yeah,' Mags said, but now she looked concerned. 'She came out about a minute later and went off after him.'

Garrow nodded. 'Can you tell us what she was wearing?'

'She had a dark hoodie on,' Mags said. 'I couldn't tell you what else.' She let out a nervous sigh. 'I never put two and two together.'

French got up from the sofa. 'Thank you. You've been very helpful.'

CHAPTER 40

Glastonbury Festival

Sunday 30 June, 2002

It was early evening and Ruth and her two friends, Katie and Ally, were making their way across the bumpy terrain of Glastonbury Festival. Now in their thirties, Ruth had known Katie and Ally since they went to sixth form college together in the late 80s. A decision had been made not to go to the Sunday afternoon slot at the Pyramid Stage. Instead, they were heading over to The Other Stage where the band *Elbow* were playing.

Ruth stopped for a moment and winced at the blisters that had developed on the heels of both feet. 'Jesus,' she grumbled as she tried to adjust her socks and her DM boots. 'Can we stop for a minute?'

'Come on,' Ally groaned. 'I don't want to miss *Elbow.*' She was wearing a bright blue bucket hat and yellow T-shirt that had *Drop Acid Not Bombs* written on it in a 70s font.

'Well go without me,' Ruth snapped as she sat down and began to unlace her boots. She pulled yet another plaster out of the numerous pockets of her long cargo shorts. The gallons of cider, mixed with minimal sleep, aching limbs and general exhaustion was making her a bit cranky.

Katie, who was wearing denim shorts and a pink cut off top, pointed to one of the many bars. 'Cider?'

Ruth and Ally nodded.

'Sorry,' Ruth said as she pulled out a cigarette and gave one to Ally.

'It's all right,' Ally said as she took it, got out a lighter and squatted down to light them both.

'Ta.' Ruth took a long drag and then let the plume of smoke escape slowly from her mouth and nose.

'I did tell you that if you were going to get new boots to wear them in,' Ally reminded her.

'Thanks Mum,' Ruth joked.

Ally gave her a sarcastic smile. 'And if we were in the army, me and Katie would be leaving you here and then you'd be taken prisoner by the Gooks and tortured. So, you should be grateful that we stopped for cider.'

Ruth shook her head. 'Yeah, I think you've watched too many Vietnam films. And you definitely can't say the word *Gooks* ever again.'

Ally looked confused. 'Why not?'

'It's a pejorative word for Vietnamese people.'

'Pejorative?' Ally rolled her eyes. 'What the hell does that mean?'

'Rude, nasty, insulting. It's like saying the 'P' word for Pakistani people,' Ruth said, now worrying that she was coming across as terribly politically correct.

'Oh right. Sorry,' Ally said, pulling a face.

Katie arrived with three plastic mugs of cider. 'Here we go.'

Ally looked at her pint. 'It's cloudy.'

'It's scrumpy,' Katie said with a knowing grin.

'Great,' Ruth laughed. 'It's basically food then.'

'Cheers,' Ally said as they raised their plastic cups.

'It's also 9 per cent alcohol so it's going to knock our bloody socks off,' Katie said.

Ruth smoothed down the fresh plasters and pulled back on her socks and boots. 'As long as it numbs my feet, I don't care.'

'Come on then,' Ally said with a smile.

Ruth hauled her rucksack, which contained water, sunglasses, cagoule and forty Marlboro Lights, onto her back.

They weaved their way through the endless stream of festivalgoers as they headed towards The Other Stage. Even though it was warm, the sky had been cloudy for most of the day. But as they reached The Other Stage the sun slowly appeared, throwing down a lovely golden light across the whole scene. There were two huge red NME signs either side of the stage that seemed to glow in the sunshine. Tall flags that carried everything from the Pride rainbow to the Welsh dragon fluttered and swayed in the wind. The air was thick with an array of smells – fried food, weed, booze, grass and the portable toilets.

Elbow were already playing when they arrived. Ruth had always thought that the band was too guitar-based for her liking but as she, Katie and Ally drank several pints of warm cider, she felt enchanted by Guy Garvey's voice.

Once the *Elbow* set had finished, Ruth and her friends set about having a rest and finding some food.

They found a spot high up that allowed them to look down and across The Other Stage in the near distance. As Ruth sat back, she looked up. The sky had started to darken and pushed back any hint of cloud. A clear indigo vista illuminated by a soft, end-of-day light.

'Want a go on this?' Katie asked, passing her a spliff.

Ruth shook her head. 'I'm all right thanks.'

Katie glanced at her knowingly. 'I wasn't sure if it was "What goes on in Glastonbury, stays in Glastonbury"?'

Ruth lifted yet another pint of scrumpy. Her head was now fuzzy. 'I'll stick to the industrial strength cider.'

Katie laughed as she puffed on the spliff.

Her friends knew that Ruth was a police officer and no longer took drugs as she had done in the early 90s.

Taking a deep breath, Ruth used the momentary pause in the day to reflect. She was thirty-five years old and a detective sergeant in London's Metropolitan Police and based in Peckham SE15. She loved her job, which she regarded as the best in the world. She was also a single mum to Ella who was now nine years old. Her mind turned to her ex-husband, Dan. At the end of the 90s, they had lived in a small ground-floor flat in a side road, halfway up Balham Hill. Five years ago, Ruth had discovered that Dan was having an affair. It had turned her world upside down. Soon after that, he had moved to Australia with his girlfriend to build a new life and rarely spoke to Ella anymore. It made Ruth both furious and sad. And she hated Dan for what he'd done to Ella. Ruth wished that she could find someone to share her life with, but she'd had a series of failed relationships.

Suddenly, the lights on the stage started to darken and a deep base noise seemed to reverberate through the air. Ruth hadn't noticed but a crowd had started to arrive for *Groove Armada*, an electronic music duo that they all really wanted to see.

Ruth saw that Katie and Ally were already up on their feet looking excited. Ally reached down, grabbed Ruth's hand and pulled her up.

'Come on,' Ally yelled gleefully. 'They're playing *Superstylin'*!'

Now feeling a little unsteady on her feet, Ruth ran with her friends down the incline and towards the crowd who had already started to whistle, cheer and jump up and down to the opening beats of the song.

When they had got as far as they could, they yelled and joined in with dancing festivalgoers. Someone nearby had a whistle which they blew rhythmically giving the atmosphere a carnival feel.

A man and a woman in their twenties came bounding over, full of energy and delight.

'Ally!' shouted the man. He was wearing round sunglasses, a pink crop top and a feather boa.

They hugged.

Ally grabbed Ruth and Katie. 'Hey, this is Richard and Sarah. I work with them.' Ally worked in health and social care. 'These are my oldest friends, Ruth and Katie!'

There were grins and nods.

Then Ruth looked at Ally's friend, Sarah. She had brunette hair in a ponytail with sunglasses perched on top. With high cheekbones and big chestnut eyes, Ruth instantly thought she was beautiful. She got a little fizz in her stomach.

Sarah looked back at her, smiled and their eyes met for a few seconds.

Oh my God, she's gorgeous.

Sarah leaned in to talk to Ruth. 'I'm sorry, I've taken a pill so my eyes must look like saucers,' she confessed with a laugh.

Ruth could smell her slightly boozy breath and perfume. She got another buzz of excitement.

'What have you taken?' Sarah asked.

Ruth held up her plastic cup of cider. 'Strictly scrumpy for me!'

'Oh, you must be the copper that Ally was telling us about,' she said as they locked eyes again and Sarah touched her arm.

Is it me, or is there something going on here?

'Guilty as charged,' Ruth joked.

Sarah laughed and then hugged her. 'It's so nice to meet you!'

Yeah, she is definitely off her face.

'You too!' Ruth said as she hugged her back, enjoying the feeling of holding her.

There was a spark of interest in Sarah's eyes as she looked at Ruth. 'You're much prettier than I imagined. Sorry, that sounds terrible.'

'It's fine,' Ruth laughed.

Sarah smiled. 'I've never met a really fit police officer before.'

Okay, I'm pretty sure she's flirting with me.

Sarah reached out, took Ruth by the hand and pulled her over to a space. They gazed at each other as they began to dance.

Sarah took Ruth's hands in hers, pulled her close, and kissed her on the mouth.

CHAPTER 41

Garrow and French came out of the front door to Mags Roseblade's flat and onto the street.

Grabbing his phone, Garrow immediately called Nick to inform him what she had told them.

'Jim?' Nick said on the other end of the phone.

'Boss,' Garrow replied. 'Mags Roseblade says that she heard Layla Hughes and Matty Hopkins arguing on Saturday night. When she heard Matty leave, she looked out of the window. Not only did she say that Matty was very unsteady on his feet, but she also watched Layla Hughes follow him.'

'Right,' Nick said thoughtfully. 'I think we've got enough to bring Layla here to officially help with our enquiries. If she doesn't play ball, arrest her.'

'Yes, boss.'

'Any idea if she's at home?'

'No. We didn't want to try until we'd spoken to you.'

'That's fine. And if she's not in, try the café and find out when she's due in for her next shift.'

'Will do.'

'Thanks, Jim,' Nick said as he ended the call.

Garrow turned his gaze to French and pointed to the bell that was marked *Flat 1a*.

'Boss wants us to bring her in now,' Garrow explained.

'Thought he might.'

French reached forwards, pressed the bell for a few seconds and then waited.

They waited for a minute before he tried the bell again. Nothing.

'Maybe we should try the café?' Garrow suggested.

'Maybe they'll do you some weird herbal tea to take away,' French joked.

Garrow gave him a wry smile as they made their way along the pavement.

A white Ford Fiesta pulled over to the pavement about fifty yards ahead of them and parked. It caught Garrow's eye as the driver's parking was both abrupt and on an angle. It seemed that whoever was driving was preoccupied or in a hurry – or both.

A figure got out.

It was Layla Hughes.

'Sarge.' Garrow gestured up the road.

'Stroke of luck,' French muttered under his breath.

As she was walking away from the car, Layla looked up and spotted them heading her way.

Shit! She's seen us.

Looking startled, she headed back and got in the driver's side.

'Bollocks,' French said, 'she's doing a runner.'

Garrow and French immediately spun around, ran back to their car and jumped in.

Garrow heard the sound of a car engine revving. He looked up and saw the Ford Fiesta pull away from the pavement at speed and then drive up the road towards them.

Turning on the ignition, French gunned the 2-litre fuel injection engine.

'Oh no, you don't,' he growled, as he started to pull their navy-coloured Astra across the road to block her path.

Garrow watched as the Fiesta started to speed up.

This is not good.

'Sarge, I don't think she's going to stop,' Garrow said uneasily.

'Yeah, we'll see about that,' French snapped as he pulled the Astra so that it was perpendicular to the road.

Garrow held his breath for a second. This was turning into a dangerous game of chicken.

The police Astra was now blocking virtually the whole road.

Surely she's going to stop now? Garrow thought to himself.

However, it was clear that Layla had no intention of stopping. Instead, she swung her Fiesta violently over to the left-hand side of the road and smashed into the front wing of their car, knocking it out of her way.

There was a huge bang inside the car and the sound of metal crunching and glass smashing.

Garrow grabbed his seat and the door as he felt his whole body jolt suddenly back and to the right.

'Fucking hell!' French yelled.

Garrow took a moment to compose himself. *Did she actually just do that?*

Then he glanced to his right and saw Layla speeding away. 'Bloody cheek!'

'Yeah, well that's an understatement,' French snarled as he jumped out of the car, raced around to look at the damage, then got back in.

'Just damage to the wing,' he said as he slammed the door aggressively.

He stamped down on the accelerator with such force that the car jolted forwards and the tyres squealed under the sudden burst of speed.

Garrow was thrown back in his seat by the force of the acceleration.

'Sarge,' Garrow said in a cautionary tone.

'What?' French replied in a mock innocent tone as he nodded to the Tetra car radio. 'Come on, Jim. Call it in!'

Grabbing the receiver, Garrow clicked the grey *Talk* button. 'Control from eight zero, are you receiving, over?'

After a few seconds there was a crackle and a female voice. 'Eight zero, this is Control, we are receiving, go ahead.'

French accelerated up to 50 mph as they sped up the road and spotted the Fiesta turning left and then disappearing.

'We're in pursuit of a white Ford Fiesta, possibly registered to a Layla Hughes,' Garrow explained as they screamed towards the junction with the main road and then came to a shuddering halt.

Please let me get out of this car in one piece.

Garrow glanced at the built-in satnav map. 'We're heading north on Princes Drive, Colwyn Bay. Request back up, over.'

'Eight zero, received, stand by,' the computer aided dispatch controller said.

Darting out onto the other side of the road, French reached over and switched on the siren and the blue lights – known as *the blues and twos* – that were located in the radiator grill.

'Right, everyone get out of my bloody way,' he said with grim determination.

A lorry tried to pull out of the petrol station to their right and French stamped on the brake and swerved left to avoid it.

Garrow was thrown hard against his seatbelt and then back by the force of French's braking.

The Fiesta was up ahead and weaving in and out of the traffic at speed.

'Bloody hell,' French said in an astounded tone. 'She's not for stopping.'

Garrow glanced at him with humour in his eyes. 'And she's surprisingly good at driving.'

French shot him a withering look. 'Jim?'

'Sarge?'

'Shut up.'

'Sarge,' Garrow said, knowing that French was half joking.

Whether or not all this was a sign that Layla Hughes was guilty of Matty Hopkins' murder, smashing into a police car and driving away was incredibly stupid.

As Garrow looked out, he saw that the Fiesta had made a very tight right-hand turn into a side road.

Without braking, French turned the steering wheel sharply to follow.

Jesus!

Garrow grabbed the seat as the tyres screeched on the road beneath them.

The Fiesta was now only twenty yards ahead of them and no match for the powerful 2-litre engine of the Astra, and French's training as an advanced pursuit driver.

Up ahead, a huge recycling lorry was coming the other way. There wasn't enough room.

The Fiesta's brake lights burned red as Layla stamped on the brakes and skidded.

For a moment, Garrow thought she was going to plough straight into the lorry. He held his breath again, but she managed to stop just in time.

Jesus that was close.

French slammed on the brakes throwing Garrow forwards. The seatbelt cut hard into his shoulder.

In the split second that they stopped, Garrow unclipped the seatbelt, threw open the door, and sprinted down towards the Fiesta.

Layla got out of the car looking shaken.

Garrow got to her and saw that she wasn't going to run. Instead she looked broken and bewildered. He took his cuffs from his belt. 'Layla Hughes, I'm arresting you for damaging police property and dangerous driving.'

CHAPTER 42

Nick and French were making their way towards the interview room where Layla Hughes and the duty solicitor were waiting.

French's mobile phone rang and he answered it. 'DS French?'

As they passed the custody suite, a shaven-headed man in his twenties was kicking off and shouting. His eyes were wild and he looked like he had taken drugs. He turned and spat at one of the uniformed officers standing behind him but luckily missed.

'Right, get him down on the ground,' a uniformed sergeant snapped.

Suddenly, three officers moved in and the man was put into a restraint, pushed to the floor and put into handcuffs in a matter of seconds.

Christ, I do not miss being in uniform, Nick thought to himself as he and French walked on. Even though CID officers did have to make arrests, the kind of aggressive and abusive behaviour they had just witnessed was a daily event for uniform. And the joke was that in a few hours the shaven-headed man would admit to taking a drug like spice and say that he had no recollection of spitting or being abusive.

French ended the phone call on his mobile and looked at Nick. 'SOCOs have entered Layla Hughes' flat to do a search.'

'Good,' Nick replied. 'Let's see what they turn up.'

'Mags Roseblade also told us that she'd spoken to Matty Hopkins a while back,' French said. 'Nothing more than passing the time of day with him when putting out the bins. Mags and Layla had been relatively close up to that point, but once she'd spoken to Matty, Layla warned her to never speak to him again. And from then on, she's completely blanked Mags.'

Nick raised an eyebrow. 'What's Mags Roseblade like?'

French shrugged. 'She's in her forties. Looks like she's just walked out of Woodstock. Objectively, Layla Hughes is an attractive looking young woman. But her jealous possessiveness is bordering on psychotic.'

'And maybe that's why she followed Matty on Saturday night and killed him?' Nick suggested as they arrived at Interview Room 2 and went in.

Layla was dressed again in a grey sweatshirt and bottoms. She glared directly at them as they crossed the room and sat down.

The duty solicitor, Amanda Price, whispered something in Layla's ear. Nick thought she might have been reminding Layla to keep calm, because she looked like a wound coil.

'Afternoon,' French said politely to Price.

'Afternoon,' she replied quietly as she looked at the documents in front of her.

'Are we all ready?' Nick asked as he shifted in his chair.

Price looked at Layla who didn't respond.

Nick leaned over and pressed the red button on the digital recording equipment. There was a long, loud electronic beep.

'Interview conducted with Layla Hughes, Interview Room 2, Llancastell Police Station. Present are Duty Solicitor Amanda Price, Detective Sergeant Daniel French, and myself, Detective Sergeant Nick Evans.'

French glanced over at her. 'Layla, do you understand that you're under arrest for damaging police property, endangering life and dangerous driving?'

Layla narrowed her eyes and gave a nonchalant shrug. 'Yeah.'

They waited for a few seconds and then French pulled his chair a little closer to the table before speaking. 'Layla, can you tell us why you rammed a police car this afternoon and then drove away at high speed?'

'I was scared,' she replied, as if this was a reasonable response.

'Why were you scared? Myself and DC Garrow hadn't even spoken to you when you saw us.'

'Because I thought you were going to frame me for Matty's murder,' she answered with a derisive snort.

Nick glanced at French. It was a strange answer to his question. But then again, Layla's behaviour had been incredibly strange all afternoon.

'I don't understand,' French said calmly. 'Why would you think that DC Garrow and I were going to "frame you" for Matty's murder?'

'That's how it works, isn't it? You've got to pin his death on someone. Why not me? The loony girlfriend.'

Nick wasn't quite sure what to make of Layla's response. He reached over and took a document from a file. 'For the purposes of the tape, I'm going to show the suspect Item Reference 230G. This is the statement you gave officers two days ago in which you stated that after you and Matty had had sex in your flat, he went back to the Pen-y-Bryn Holiday Park, and you stayed in your flat for the rest of the night and until the following day. Is that correct?'

Layla furrowed her brow and looked angry. 'Yes, that is correct.'

Nick gave her a quizzical look. 'Would it surprise you to know that we have an eyewitness who saw you following Matty once he had left your flat? Is there anything you can tell us about that?'

'Who?' Layla snapped.

'Please answer the question, Layla,' French said wearily. 'Did you follow Matty when he left your flat?'

'No, of course not,' she said sharply, and then looked at Price as if to say 'What the hell are they talking about? I didn't go anywhere.'

'So, this eyewitness is lying to us?' Nick suggested. 'Because they were very certain that they saw you following Matty on the road that leads back up to the holiday park. And they had no reason to lie to us about that.'

'God, is it that bitch that lives upstairs from me? She's got it in for me so I wouldn't believe a bloody word she says. She'd make up any old shit to make me look bad.'

French glanced at her from under lowered brows. 'Are you denying that you left the flat to follow Matty last Saturday night?'

'Yes. I didn't go anywhere. I've told you that already. I'm not lying,' Layla said adamantly.

There were a few seconds of silence.

Layla clearly wasn't going to admit that she had left the flat that night to follow Matty. It was time to move the interview on.

'Layla, do you know a Zoe Solomon?' Nick asked.

'Jesus, she's another one,' Layla scoffed. 'What the fuck did she have to say about me?'

'I take it that you *do* know Zoe Solomon?'

'Yes,' she sneered.

'Can you tell us how you know her?' French asked.

'We used to work together.'

'At the Pen-y-Bryn Holiday Park, is that correct?' Nick enquired.

'Yes, that is *correct*,' Layla said, sounding as if she was mocking Nick.

Nick sat forwards in his chair. 'But you don't work at the holiday park anymore, do you Layla?'

For a moment, Layla looked embarrassed by Nick's question. 'No,' she said defensively.

French turned the page of the notepad where he was taking notes. 'Can you tell us why you don't work there anymore?'

'Because that bitch sacked me,' she said with a huff.

French frowned. 'Are you referring to Jane Hopkins?'

'Yeah.'

Nick scratched his jawline for a second and then said, 'Can you tell us why you were sacked from the holiday park?'

'That Jane didn't like her "precious" son seeing someone like me. I wasn't good enough for him,' she said in a derisive tone. 'So, she sacked me so we couldn't be together at work.'

Nick gave her a questioning look. 'That's not what Jane or Zoe told us. In fact, they were very clear that you had physically attacked Zoe because she slept with Matty and that you believed that you were in a relationship with him.'

'Hang on! I *was* in a relationship with Matty!' she stated angrily.

French gave her a doubting look. 'Really?'

'Yes,' she said, blinking with incredulity at the question.

'That's not the picture we're getting I'm afraid, Layla,' Nick said. 'In fact, I think that you wanted to be in a relationship with Matty, but he wasn't interested. Is that right?'

'No! That is not right!' she snapped. Her face was now flushed with rage.

'I think you were obsessed with him,' Nick continued. He then reached over for a folder. 'For the purposes of the tape, I'm showing the suspect Item Reference 392H. This is a photograph taken last Thursday night that we retrieved from Matty Hopkins' phone. Can you take a look at the photo for me please, Layla?'

'Jesus, what now?' She gave an audible sigh as she peered over.

'Can you tell me what you can see in this photo please?' Nick asked.

'I can't see anything,' Layla answered with an irritated huff.

'The photograph shows a person standing outside Matty's caravan. And that person is clearly you. Is there anything you can tell us about that Layla?'

'I went to talk to him, that's all,' she said. 'He's my boyfriend. And I'm allowed to talk to my boyfriend, aren't I?'

French waited for a few seconds, then said, 'I'm confused. You've just told us that you were in a relationship with Matty. Why are you standing outside his caravan in the dark? And why did he text you later that evening to tell you to leave him alone or he would call the police?'

'We were just having a few problems, that's all.' Layla gave a fake laugh. 'Classic Matty. It was all about the drama.'

'Come on, Layla,' Nick said forcefully. 'You were never in a relationship with Matty. You had sex every now and then. And you wanted it to be more, but he was just not interested. In fact, he was more interested in having sex with other female members of staff who lived on site at the park. And that made you jealous and very angry, didn't it?'

'No. That's not true,' she snapped angrily. 'You can't say stuff like that about him!'

'In fact, you were so angry that you decided to follow him when he left your flat. You watched him go into that cabin. You knew where the keys were kept from when you worked there, so you took the keys to Cabin 5 and locked Matty in there. Then you took petrol from one of the maintenance sheds and set the cabin on fire, didn't you?'

'No!' Layla screeched as she stood up and her chair flew back.

For a second, she just glared across the table, breathing heavily, with her fists clenched.

'Please sit down Layla,' Nick said abruptly.

Price reached up and touched Layla's arm to indicate that she needed to sit down. Layla let out a frustrated growl and sat back in her seat.

'You need to explain what happened when you followed Matty up to the park,' French said.

'Nothing,' Layla replied. 'I didn't follow him.'

'We know that you did, Layla,' Nick said.

'Okay, okay, so what if I followed Matty?' she said, gesturing with her hands. 'He was being a twat. I followed him. So what?'

French stopped writing and looked over at her. 'And you followed him all the way up to the holiday park?'

She shook her head. 'No. As I started to calm down, I realised that there was no point. So I turned around and went back to my flat.'

'You really expect us to believe that?' French asked curtly.

Layla shrugged. 'It's the truth.'

Nick sat back in his seat and looked at her for a moment. 'I assume that you had your phone with you when you decided to follow Matty?'

Layla looked confused. 'Yeah, I must have done.'

'Your phone gives off a GPS signal when it's on,' he explained. 'And that means we can track your phone's movements on Saturday night. Would you like to tell us what really happened when you followed Matty up to the park?'

'I'm not lying to you,' Layla said through gritted teeth.

There was a knock at the door and Garrow stuck his head in and looked over.

'Boss, I need a word,' he said quietly.

Nick got up. He knew it had to be important for Garrow to call him out of an interview.

'For the purposes of the tape, DS Evans is leaving the interview room,' French said as Nick went to the door.

Garrow pulled out his phone as he and Nick went into the corridor.

'What is it, Jim?' Nick asked.

'The forensic team just sent me this,' Garrow explained as he showed Nick a photograph.

It was a small bottle of clear liquid with a bright orange sticker that read *GHB – Liquid Ecstasy – Avoid Alcohol*.

Nick puffed his cheeks and then exhaled. 'Looks like she's the one that drugged Matty. Can you send me that photo right now?'

'Yes, boss,' Garrow said as he tapped at his phone.

'Thanks, Jim.'

Nick marched back into the interview room and headed back to his seat. This was the kind of breakthrough that they had been looking for in the investigation.

'For the purposes of the tape, DS Evans has re-entered the interview room,' French said.

Nick waited for a few seconds and then gave Layla a quizzical look as he took out his phone.

'What?' Layla snarled defensively.

Looking down at his phone, Nick pulled up the photo that Garrow had sent him.

'My forensic team are currently searching your flat,' he informed her.

'Good. I've got nothing to hide.'

Nick looked at her directly. 'Layla, can you take a look at this photograph for me please?'

He turned the phone to show her. She frowned, looked over, and then the colour visibly drained from her face.

She shrugged. 'So what?'

Nick took the phone back. 'Can you tell me what you can see in that photograph, please?'

'It's not mine,' she said with a disdainful expression.

'For the purposes of the tape, I have shown the suspect a bottle of the drug GHB that has been discovered at her flat by the forensic team,' Nick stated. 'Can you tell me why you have a bottle of GHB in your possession?'

'I told you, it's not mine,' she insisted.

'Who does it belong to then?' Nick asked.

'I don't know.'

Nick took a breath. 'GHB was classified as an illegal substance under the Misuse of Drugs Act of 1971. Therefore, it is a criminal offence to have it in your possession at your flat. Is there anything you'd like to say about that?'

'No,' Layla muttered under her breath, but her brusque attitude had been replaced by fear.

French fixed her with a stare. 'Would it surprise you to know that in the post-mortem, traces of GHB were found in Matty's blood?'

Layla's body language had become closed off and she bit nervously at her nails. 'What's that got to do with me?'

'Did you give Matty GHB when he was at your flat on Saturday night?' French asked forcefully.

'No,' Layla said, shaking her head, but she wasn't doing a very good job of hiding the fact that she was lying.

'Really?' French said with an unconvinced expression.

'No.'

'Don't you think it's an extraordinary coincidence that Matty came to your flat where you have the drug GHB. *And after his death, he was found to have taken GHB.* But it had nothing to do with you?'

Layla didn't respond.

'Did you spike Matty's drink when he was at your flat, Layla?' Nick asked in a calm tone.

'No,' Layla replied, but she sounded rattled.

'You didn't want Matty to leave after you'd had sex, did you?' French suggested. 'So, you spiked his drink with GHB in the hope that he'd pass out, but he didn't. When he left your flat, you followed him up to the holiday park where you killed him. Isn't that right?'

'No,' Layla sobbed as she shook her head. 'No, that's not what happened.' She then buried her head in her hands.

'I think my client needs a break,' the duty solicitor suggested calmly.

Nick nodded.

CHAPTER 43

While Layla Hughes was taking a break in the custody holding cells, Nick sat in the main meeting room opposite Geraldine Burrows – forties, brunette, intelligent, business-like – who worked for the CPS in North Wales. They had been discussing the evidence that they had against Layla and whether or not it met the threshold for them to charge her with Matty Hopkins' murder. Nick knew it was going to be a stretch, but he felt it was worth having the conversation and keeping the CPS in the loop.

Burrows turned a page from a manilla evidence folder and then pulled a face. 'To be honest Nick, we're getting hammered with budget cuts. There's pressure from the DPP all the way down the chain of command to hold back on taking anything risky to trial.'

The DPP is the Director of Public Prosecutions who is essentially the head of the Crown Prosecution Service. He is the third most senior public prosecutor in England and Wales after the attorney general and solicitor general.

'Of course,' Nick said in an understanding tone. Since he joined the police force in 2003, there had been a 25 per cent cut in police budgets in real terms and the closure of hundreds of police stations.

'Our conviction rate dropped down to 77 per cent last year,' Burrows explained. 'Five years ago it was 84 per cent.' She then looked back at the folder. 'Everything you've got is circumstantial. Until I can see something linking Layla Hughes to the fire, I can't see how you've met the threshold to charge her with murder.'

'I understand,' Nick said calmly. That had been his initial instinct, but he'd learned from Ruth to keep the CPS fully informed of the progress of something as major as a murder investigation.

Burrows got up from her seat and began to gather her stuff.

'You got married?' Nick said, pointing to a new engagement and wedding ring on her finger.

'Yes,' Burrows laughed. She seemed bemused by his observation.

'Sorry, force of habit,' Nick explained and then realised his faux pas. 'God, I don't mean that I check out the marital status of every woman I meet. It's just as a detective, I notice stuff like that. Goes with the job, I suppose.'

Burrows smiled at him as she put on her designer coat. 'So, what you're saying is that you do actually check out the marital status of every woman you meet?'

Nick took a moment and gave her a wry smile. 'Yes. And every man. And I notice if someone has had a manicure, or if they're right-handed or left-handed, and have clear or bloodshot eyes. And so it goes on. Gets a bit wearing but it's instinctive now.'

Before Burrows could say anything the door opened and Georgie looked in. She was holding a laptop. 'Can I have a word?' she said.

Nick got up and nodded. 'We were just finishing up here. This is Geraldine Burrows from the CPS. DC Georgie Wild.'

'Hi there,' Georgie said. 'Actually this might be something that Geraldine should see too.'

'Okay,' Nick said as he looked over to Burrows.

'Fine by me,' she said, sitting down again as Georgie came in, sat down and opened up the laptop.

'What have we got?' Nick asked, now intrigued. If Georgie felt Burrows should take a look then it had to be significant.

'I've found something on the CCTV from the holiday park,' Georgie explained as she tapped away on the keyboard.

Nick and Burrows leaned in to look at the laptop screen.

'Okay, so we looked at all the CCTV in the area of the luxury cabins and came up with nothing. It was either too dark, or the cameras just didn't cover the area we wanted to look at,' Georgie said. 'I'm aware that Layla Hughes is our prime suspect, so I've just taken a look at the approach road that comes in from the woods. And I found this.'

Nick peered at the screen as the CCTV played. At first, all he could see was the road with a bank of dark trees behind that were swaying in the wind. But then a figure appeared walking along. Georgie paused the image. She gestured to the timecode at the bottom. 'This person arrives at the park at 11:43 p.m.,' she explained. She then zoomed in to the frozen image.

Nick did a double take. The figure on the road was carrying what looked like two petrol cans. However, the image was heavily pixelated and fuzzy.

'You can see that whoever it is, they're wearing a black baseball cap,' Georgie said.

'But you can't see their face,' Nick said, a little disappointed.

Burrows frowned. 'Is that the best quality we can get on that?'

'It is at the moment, I'm afraid,' Georgie admitted. 'The guys in digital forensics said they don't have the equipment to enhance it here. They can send it over to Manchester where they do, but that can take up to a week.'

Nick shrugged. 'Let's get it done, however long it takes.'

'Yes, boss. But we do also have this…' Georgie said as she clicked the laptop again. The image of a black baseball cap in an evidence bag came onto the screen. It had *Pen-y-Bryn Holiday Park* written on it in green writing like the one he'd seen the Park Manager, Dylan Williams, wearing.

'What's that?' Burrows asked.

'It's a Pen-y-Bryn Holiday Park baseball cap that forensics found in Layla Hughes' flat,' Georgie told her. She then pointed back at the image on her laptop. 'It looks a lot like the one this person is wearing.'

Nick took a moment to process this. 'The thing is, I think those baseball caps are fairly popular with members of staff. It doesn't narrow it down,' he said.

He could see that Georgie was a little disappointed.

'Sorry,' Nick said. 'This is great work, Georgie.' He then gave Burrows a quizzical look. 'I just don't think it gets us over the CPS threshold.'

'No, it doesn't,' Burrows conceded as she looked at them. 'Tell you what. If that image does turn out to be Layla Hughes, I can take another look at charging her with Matty Hopkins' murder. We're very close, so just hang on in there.'

CHAPTER 44

Walking along the hospital corridor, Nick tried to process the past few hours. The FME – the forensic medical examiner – had checked Layla Hughes and confirmed that she was fit to be held overnight at Llancastell nick. She was clearly their prime suspect, and they could interview her again in the morning. A night in the cells might frighten her enough to start telling the truth.

As Nick made his way along the corridor, he felt a growing sense of dread at seeing Ruth after Sarah had called him that morning. He just needed to lower his expectations and prepare himself.

As he turned the corner into the ward, he saw Ella and Sarah standing outside Ruth's room with a doctor. They were deep in discussion. At first, Nick's stomach tightened as he worried that something terrible had happened. But he could tell from their expressions that whatever was concerning them, it wasn't catastrophic.

The doctor left as Nick approached.

'Hi, Nick,' Sarah said as she came over and hugged him.

'Hi,' he said as Ella gave him a hug too. He gestured to the doctor who was walking away down the corridor. 'Everything all right?'

Sarah looked uneasy. 'It's like I told you this morning. She keeps coming in and out of consciousness. And when she does come round, she…' Sarah's eyes filled with tears.

Nick put a comforting hand on her arm. 'What did the doctor say?'

Ella looked at him. 'He said we have to be patient. Apparently being irritable, confused and having memory problems can be a side effect of being in an induced coma.'

Nick nodded and then gestured to the door. 'Do you mind if I go in and see her?'

Sarah wiped the tears from her face. 'Of course not.'

'She's asleep at the moment,' Ella explained, as they opened the door slowly and went inside.

Nick looked over at the bed where Ruth was lying. For a moment, he felt overwhelmed at seeing her so helpless and vulnerable.

He went over to a grey plastic chair on the far side of her bed and sat down.

For the next few minutes, they all sat in silence.

Then Ruth started to stir. Her face twisted slightly with a confused frown and her eyes blinked open a little.

Sarah got up, went over to the bedside cabinet and took a plastic beaker of water. She went over to Ruth and put the beaker close to her mouth.

'Hi Ruth,' she said in a virtual whisper. 'Do you want some water?'

Ruth lashed out and hit the beaker flying. 'No, I don't want any fucking water!' she snapped. 'What are you trying to do to me anyway?'

Sarah wiped the water from her face. Then she pointed at Nick. 'Ruth?'

'What?' Ruth replied with an angry expression.

'Looks who's come to see you,' Sarah said very gently. 'It's Nick. Do you remember Nick? You work together.'

'Don't be ridiculous,' Ruth thundered as she turned and glared at Nick. 'Who the hell are you?'

Nick was shocked and unsettled by Ruth's appearance and behaviour. It was upsetting to see her twisted face and her eyes glowering at him. He'd never seen her like this before. It seemed as if she'd been possessed by a completely different person.

'It's Nick,' he said gently. 'How are you feeling?'

Ruth looked repelled by him as she glanced at Ella. 'Who is this man?'

'Nick,' Ella said, trying to be patient.

'Well I want him out of here,' Ruth growled. 'He has no business being in here. Who the hell does he think he is?'

Nick stood up slowly and looked at Ella and Sarah.

'Get out! All of you!' Ruth screamed loudly. 'I want all of you out of here now!'

CHAPTER 45

Nick shifted himself back on Megan's pink duvet as he turned the page of the book that he'd been reading to her. Her bedside lamp and the string of twinkling fairy lights on the wall behind her bed gave the room a lovely warm glow. Nick had been known to nod off on her bed and have to be woken up by Amanda when she eventually wondered where he'd disappeared to.

He turned a page and continued to read from Megan's latest book about a time travelling dragon called Kevin. 'What time do you call this, Kevin? You're lucky that I've kept your tea warm,' Nick said. 'Sorry, I got a bit tied up, Mum.' Nick turned the final page. 'Well go and wash your hands then... Kevin rolled his eyes. If only she knew that he'd just saved the world from alien invasion.'

Closing the book, Nick leaned over and kissed Megan on the forehead. For a second, he saw how much she looked like Amanda. The same big brown eyes and cute button nose. He was filled with a sense of gratitude for what he had. It wasn't that long ago that he'd nearly lost everything. Nick knew that he needed to constantly remind himself of everything that he had in his life. A beautiful healthy daughter and wife. A roof over his head and money to pay the bills and buy food. A job that he loved. And ongoing sobriety. He needed to remember that there were so many people out there who didn't have all of those things and not take them for granted. As the old AA adage said, *A grateful alcoholic won't drink*.

Megan smiled at him and then frowned with a quizzical expression that wrinkled her nose. 'When is Auntie Ruth coming over again? I want to see her.'

Nick took a moment as he wondered how best to answer her question.

'Actually, Auntie Ruth isn't very well at the moment,' he said lightly.

'Has she got a cold?' Megan asked.

'Sort of, but I'm sure she'll be better soon,' he reassured her.

'Harry Davies in my class had a cold and he was off school for a whole week,' she said.

'Was he?' Nick said as he moved himself off the bed. 'Well, when Auntie Ruth is better, she can come over for Sunday lunch, okay?'

'Okay…' Megan yawned and put her head onto the pillow, '…but only if Mummy cooks.'

'What?' Nick said with a mock indignation and then a smile. 'What's wrong with my cooking?'

Megan gave a little shrug. 'I prefer Mummy's.'

'Right, I see. Well I can't fault you for your honesty. Love you, sweetpea,' he whispered as he went towards the door.

'Love you, Daddy,' she replied, but her eyes were already closed and her hand had moved up to the side of her face which is how she slept every night.

Padding down the landing, Nick tried to process what had happened at the hospital.

He came down the stairs, along the hallway and into the living room.

Amanda was sitting reading in the armchair.

'Is she okay?' Amanda asked, taking off her reading glasses.

'Apparently she prefers your cooking to mine,' he said with a wry smile.

'Erm, of course she does,' Amanda laughed.

'She asked when she could see Auntie Ruth.'

'Oh.' Amanda got up from the armchair and went over to him. She put her arms around him and they hugged. 'I know it must have been horrible to see Ruth like that, but people do recover. It just takes time.'

'But what if she doesn't recover?' Nick sighed. 'What if she has brain damage and that's just her now?'

He walked over to the sofa and slumped down. He felt lost.

Amanda looked at her watch. 'Why don't you go to a meeting?'

Nick knew that she was probably right. Going to an AA meeting, sharing how he was feeling and connecting with other alcoholics might be exactly what he needed.

'Do you mind?' he asked.

Amanda rolled her eyes. 'I just suggested it, stupid. Isn't there a meeting in Mold tonight?'

Nick nodded. Mold was about a half hour drive away.

She came over and took his hand. 'Come on. Off you go. We can have some dinner together when you get back.'

Nick got up and gave her kiss. 'Thank you.'

CHAPTER 46

It was eight a.m. and Nick perched himself on a desk in the CID office. He waited for a moment for everyone to settle. Going to an AA meeting the night before had definitely helped clear his head and given him perspective and some semblance of peace. AA meetings usually ended with everyone saying the serenity prayer. *God, grant me the serenity to accept the things I cannot change, change the things I can, and the wisdom to know the difference.* Like many in AA, Nick wasn't religious in any formal way. But the realisation that he wasn't able to control many things in his life was always a useful thing to remember.

'Okay everyone,' he said tentatively. 'The good news is that the boss has now come out of the induced coma. And I went to see her last night. She is still very disorientated, and her memory is a bit foggy, but the doctors have said that this is to be expected.' He wasn't about to describe the disturbing events of the previous evening to the CID team. 'So, I'll keep you updated on her progress as and when I hear anything.'

Nick could see the impact that Ruth's shooting and ongoing ill health was having on the team. She had been their leader for nearly five years, and it was unsettling not to have her presence in the room. He went over to the scene board, waited for a moment, and then said, 'Okay, we have arrested Layla Hughes for the murder of Matty

Hopkins. She is currently downstairs in a custody cell and we will be interviewing her again this morning.' He glanced at his watch. 'However, we have until five p.m. this afternoon to charge her or she will be released. What have we got?'

Georgie looked over. 'Still waiting on digital forensics in Manchester to clean up that CCTV, boss. I've pushed, but it's going to take days rather than hours.'

'Okay,' Nick said, feeling frustrated. 'What about Layla's mobile phone?'

French sat forwards in his seat. 'Digital forensics have that too, boss. I've asked them to track the GPS signal from her phone last Saturday night. I'm hoping that will show that she followed Matty from Colwyn Bay up to the holiday park and possibly that she was close to Cabin 5 when it was set on fire.'

'Thanks, Dan,' Nick said. 'What about the memory stick I got from Matty's caravan?'

'The files were encrypted, boss,' Garrow explained as he pointed towards his computer. 'I've just got the decrypted version back which has the data back to its original format.'

'Anything?' Nick asked.

'Looks like hundreds of photographs,' Garrow replied. 'I'm just starting to trawl through them, but there's nothing of interest yet.'

'Did we get anything back on the accident that Matty had three years ago?' Nick asked as he looked at some writing on the scene board.

'I'm waiting for hospital records to get back to me,' Georgie announced. 'I'll give them a chase.'

'Might be worth contacting Colwyn Bay Police and see if they attended Matty's accident,' Nick said, thinking out loud. 'Given his injuries, I'm assuming that police officers went to the scene and made some kind of report. It's probably not relevant, but just worth ticking off.'

'Will do,' Georgie confirmed.

'There is something else,' French said, looking down at a printout. 'Kevin Ball has a string of convictions for arson from when he was a teenager. They didn't come up on the PNC. They were removed because of his age when the crimes were committed. I don't know if that's relevant?'

'I guess we'll keep it in mind,' Nick said. 'But Layla Hughes is our prime suspect. So I want us to look at everything in her life, every shred of evidence, phone calls, anything. I do *not* want her waltzing out of here this afternoon.'

CHAPTER 47

'For the purposes of the tape, I am showing the suspect Item Reference 384J,' Nick said as he moved the laptop around.

Layla Hughes, who was still dressed in a grey sweatshirt and bottoms, was sitting next to the duty solicitor, Amanda Price.

Layla looked down at the floor with a sullen look on her face.

'Layla?' Nick said, raising his voice a little. 'Can you look at the CCTV footage on this laptop please?'

With an audible sigh, Layla slowly looked over and then shrugged. 'What?' she snapped.

Nick ignored her and pressed play. The dark CCTV footage played and the figure on the access road to the holiday park entered the screen.

'You see this figure here?' French asked her as Nick paused the footage.

She pulled a face as if they were being ridiculous. 'Yeah.'

'This person is entering the holiday park via the access road,' French said as he pointed at the screen. 'And these woods here are a cut through to Colwyn Bay, aren't they?'

Layla glared at him. 'No idea.'

'Come on, Layla,' Nick said, rolling his eyes. 'You know full well that there is a cut through between Colwyn Bay and the Pen-y-Bryn site.'

'I don't! How would I know?' she said with an icy stare. 'I always drive.'

French pointed to the screen again. 'This person here has two cans of petrol. Can you see that?'

Layla gave them a bemused smile. 'Yeah, so what?'

'This is you, isn't it?' French asked.

'No, of course it's not,' she protested. 'It doesn't look anything like me.'

'We're in the process of getting this CCTV footage digitally enhanced,' Nick explained.

'That's nice for you,' she sneered.

'And when we get it back…' he continued, '…we're going to see that this person is you. You were obsessed with Matty Hopkins, weren't you?'

'No. I loved him.'

'And you hated any woman who even spoke to him. You drugged him with GHB on Saturday night, but it wasn't enough to stop him leaving your flat. So, in a fit of rage, you followed him up to the holiday park. You saw him stagger into Cabin 5 where he passed out. You took the keys out of the door, shut it, and locked him in from the outside. You went and got petrol, poured it over the door and steps, and burned down that cabin with Matty inside it, didn't you?'

'Brilliant.' Layla gave a slow, sarcastic hand clap. 'You two should write books, you know that?'

French gestured to the screen again. 'This person here is wearing a black baseball cap. Do you own a black baseball cap, Layla?'

'No,' she snorted.

French reached over to a file and pulled out a photograph. 'For the purposes of the tape, I'm showing the suspect Item Reference 982B.' He turned the photo so that Layla could see it. 'Can you tell us what you can see in this photo please, Layla?'

Layla peered at it and then shrugged.

'Would it surprise you to know that this black baseball cap was found during a search of your flat? Is there anything you can tell us about that?' French enquired.

'Jesus,' Layla laughed. 'That's one of those horrible Pen-y-Bryn Holiday Park caps. They gave me that when I worked there but I wouldn't be seen dead in it.'

'But you just told us that you don't own a black baseball cap,' Nick pointed out.

'Yeah, well I forgot about that horrible thing,' she said, but then she frowned. 'Did you say that the cabin was set on fire using petrol?'

Nick looked at her. 'I'm not sure what the relevance of that is.'

'If you're looking for someone who has access to cans of petrol, you wanna ask the park's head of maintenance,' she suggested.

'And who's that?'

'Kevin Ball,' she said, raising an eyebrow.

Nick looked at French. Layla was clearly trying to implicate anyone she could think of to take the focus off her.

CHAPTER 48

Ten minutes later, Nick and French walked out of the interview room and along the busy ground floor corridor as they headed back to CID. Layla Hughes would continue to be held in a custody holding cell until her twenty-four hours lapsed or they found enough evidence to charge her with Matty's murder.

'What did you think?' Nick asked.

French tilted his head in query. 'How do you mean?'

'Kevin Ball?'

They reached the back staircase and went up.

'Layla's desperate attempt to throw him under the bus,' French answered.

'That was my thought too. She has the means, motive and opportunity. I don't think we need to look at anyone else, do we?'

'No,' French agreed adamantly.

As they entered the CID office, Nick noticed that both Garrow and Georgie had concerned expressions on their faces.

'Everything all right?' he asked as he approached where they were sitting looking at Georgie's computer screen.

Garrow gave him a dubious look. 'Not really, boss.'

'What's going on?'

He held up a printout with a map on it. 'This is from digital forensics. It's the GPS trace on Layla Hughes' phone.'

Nick was already starting to feel uneasy. 'Okay, what's the issue?'

'According to the trace, Layla followed Matty for about two minutes before turning around and heading back to her flat for the rest of the night.'

'Shit!' Nick sighed under his breath.

'It means that she didn't follow him up to the holiday park as we assumed,' Georgie said.

Nick shook his head in frustration. 'It also gives her an alibi for the time of his death.'

Georgie pointed to her computer. 'There's something else.'

Nick came around to look at what was on the screen. There was an image of two people having sex.

'Most of the photos on that memory stick are of Matty Hopkins having sex with various women,' Georgie told him. 'Which is why it was hidden under that lamp.'

Garrow indicated the image in front of them. 'And this is Matty having sex with Kat Mount.'

'What?' Nick said as he processed this.

Georgie glanced sideways at him. 'It happened ten days ago.'

Nick paused in thought for a moment before speaking. 'If Kevin Ball knew that Matty had slept with his girl-friend...'

'...then maybe he killed him?' Georgie said, finishing his sentence.

'Possibly,' Nick said, trying to get his head around the new evidence. Up until two minutes ago, Layla Hughes had been their prime suspect.

'It might explain why Miles Hopkins had to pull Matty and Kevin apart,' Garrow said.

Nick nodded. It was a good point. 'Hopkins said it was about ten days ago so that would fit in timewise.'

'It also explains why Ball lied about going back to the caravan to get vodka,' Georgie said. 'And why he then disappeared until the morning.'

'Christ,' Nick sighed as he sat down on a chair for a second. Then he looked at them. 'We have to release Layla. And we need to find Kevin Ball and bring him in.'

He rubbed his beard thoughtfully. To say that the investigation had taken a new turn was an understatement.

CHAPTER 49

An hour later, Nick and French were marching down through the static caravans as they headed for where they knew Kat Mount and Kevin Ball lived. Above them the sky was full of light, clear of clouds and a rich azure colour. The soft breath of the breeze was broken by the caw of gulls who sounded as if they were squawking a warning of their imminent arrival.

Arriving at the caravan, Nick got the distinct smell of weed. He banged on the flimsy door.

After a few seconds, it opened and Kat peered out. She had a swollen black eye and was pressing a cold tea towel against a cut on her lip.

'Are you okay?' Nick asked with concern.

'Do I look bloody okay?' she snapped at him as she dabbed her lip.

'We're looking for Kevin,' Nick explained.

'You're a bit late,' Kat sneered at him. 'You've missed him.'

'Did he do that to you?' French enquired.

'Yes,' she said, rolling her eyes as if that was a ridiculous question.

French looked more closely at her. 'You might need a stitch or two in that lip.'

'I'll be fine,' she huffed as she went to shut the door in their faces.

French reached out and stopped the door with his hand. They weren't finished with her yet.

Nick asked, 'Has Kevin gone up to the main site?'

'No, of course not.' Kat shook her head and gave him a meaningful look. 'He's gone… gone.'

'What do you mean?'

'I mean, first he did this to me,' she sighed angrily as she pointed to her face. 'Then he took all his stuff, took my car keys and stole my car. I tried to stop him but…'

'Any idea where he's going?' French said.

'Nope,' she snorted, 'and I don't bloody care.'

'We're going to need your car's registration, make, model and colour,' Nick said. He started to wonder if Kevin's sudden disappearance was a sign of his guilt.

'It's a white Ford Focus. Fuck, I'll need to look up the number plate, I've forgotten it.'

'That's fine,' French said.

'Any idea why he left in such a hurry?' Nick asked.

'No,' Kat said, but it was clear she was lying.

He stared at her for a long moment. 'We know about you and Matty.'

Kat pulled a face. 'No idea what you're talking about.'

'We've seen the photos,' French explained. 'We know you slept together.'

'Is that why Kevin did that to you?' Nick asked.

Kat looked at them and nodded but didn't say anything.

'When did he find out you and Matty had been together?' Nick asked, trying to piece everything together. If it wasn't until today then Kevin wouldn't have had a motive to murder Matty.

'The day after it happened,' she said quietly.

'And when was that?'

'About a week or ten days ago,' she said uncertainly. 'I dunno.'

Nick took a moment and then asked, 'Did Kevin murder Matty out of revenge?'

'I've no idea. Maybe. He had those burns on his hands. He disappeared. And when he found out I'd slept with Matty, he said he wanted to kill him. But I thought he was just saying it.'

Nick furrowed his brow. 'So why did all this blow up today if it happened ten days ago?'

'We haven't really spoken since,' she said. 'Kev was giving me the silent treatment. We had a row about an hour ago and I told him Matty was much better in bed than him. Kev completely lost it.'

'Does he have family in North Wales?' French asked.

'Yeah, his mum lives over in Bethesda. Patricia. She's welcome to him.'

'Have you got her address?' French enquired.

'No,' she snorted.

Nick looked at her. 'We're going to need that registration.' He looked at French. 'And then we need to get to Bethesda.'

CHAPTER 50

Nick and French were hammering east from the Colwyn Bay area towards Bethesda, which was on the edge of Snowdonia. Its ancient name was *Cilfoden* and the town was famous for its slate quarrying, especially the Penrhyn Quarry.

French took a long bend at speed.

They had given Kat's car details to central control at Llancastell dispatch and now every police car in North Wales was on the lookout for her white Ford Focus.

The car radio crackled. 'Three six from control, are you receiving, over?'

Nick took the radio. 'Control, this is three six, we are receiving, over.'

'We have a possible sighting of target vehicle heading south of the A470 close to Tal-y-Cafn, over.'

'Received. Request backup units to proceed to the A470, over,' Nick said, calculating that they were about five miles away from Tal-y-Cafn themselves.

'Understood three six, stand by.'

French glanced over. 'Looks like Ball is going cross-country to avoid the expressway.'

'Yeah,' Nick said. 'That's because he's worried we're looking for him.'

'Are we completely ruling out Layla Hughes as a suspect now?' French asked as they drove over the brow of a hill.

'I had her down as our prime suspect,' Nick admitted. 'But if we go on her mobile phone GPS, she went back to her flat before the fire started and Matty was killed, and she stayed there. We have to go with the evidence.'

'Unless someone else had her phone,' French suggested.

'She had an accomplice?' Nick asked. It wasn't something he'd considered.

'I'm just thinking out loud,' French conceded. 'My instinct was that she was so angry and deluded that it had to be her.'

'Maybe we just got it wrong,' Nick said with a shrug. 'If Layla had deliberately contrived to give us a fake GPS trace, that would mean she was fully aware that after Matty's murder we would be tracing the GPS from her phone. And that means she got someone else to deliberately take her phone back to her flat.'

'Which is a possibility,' French pointed out.

'It is,' Nick said, 'but given that she had a blazing row with Matty that night, she allowed herself to be spotted following him, and she kept hold of the GHB that she'd spiked him with in her flat, I don't give her the credit for being that smart or ingenious.'

'Fair point.'

'For my money, Matty went to Layla's flat where she spiked his drink in the hope that he passed out and stayed the night. Instead, he staggered back up to the holiday park. He felt dreadful and decided to crash out in the comfort of a vacant luxury cabin. But Kevin Ball spotted him, and in a fit of rage decided to get revenge for Matty sleeping with Kat, locked him in and torched the cabin.'

'Now you've put it like that, boss,' French said, '…that seems more plausible.'

They continued to speed along the country roads, overtaking where they could. Nick knew he was in good hands as French had taken the same advanced police driving course at the Driving Training Unit in Preston.

For a second, his thoughts turned to Ruth and what he'd witnessed at the hospital the night before. It made him shudder.

However, as he glanced up he saw a white Ford Focus pull out of a petrol station up ahead.

'Is that him?' Nick said out loud.

French peered ahead but there was an articulated lorry between them and the Ford Focus.

'Could be,' French said, his eyes locked on the road.

Glancing down at his phone, Nick pulled up the registration that Kat Mount had given them – *LV11 TOB*.

The lorry was going painfully slow and Nick worried that if it was Kevin Ball in the car, they might lose him.

'Think you can get round it?' Nick said, referring to the lorry.

With a quick flick of the steering wheel, French pulled the car out by a few feet.

'Shit!' He gasped with a wince as he pulled the car back rapidly as a car towing a caravan came the other way.

'Bollocks,' Nick muttered.

The lorry started to indicate left and gradually pulled into a layby where there was a mobile van selling coffees and burgers.

Pushing down on the accelerator, French sped up behind the Ford Focus so that they could see the plate.

LV11 TOB! Bingo.

'Got him,' Nick said. He grabbed the Tetra radio. 'Dispatch from three six. We are in pursuit of suspect Kevin Ball in a white Ford Focus, registration Lima, Victor, one, one, Tango, Oscar, Bravo. Heading south on the A470. Requesting backup, over.'

'Dispatch received three six,' the computer aided dispatch (CAD) operator replied. 'Stand by.'

Hitting the accelerator hard, French screeched around the corner.

'Don't lose him, Dan.' Nick could feel the adrenaline pumping.

'No chance,' French reassured him as he worked through the gears.

The Ford Focus was about fifty yards ahead of them as they thundered north. Glancing over to the dashboard, Nick could see that they were up to 70 mph already. He gripped the door handle with one hand and the front of his seat with the other as they screamed around a long curve in the road.

'Yeah, he's definitely spotted us, boss,' French said.

As they hit 80 mph, Nick could see they were gaining ground. As they rounded another bend, their wheels squealed as the car struggled to grip the road. Hitting the straight, the car was now only twenty yards ahead of them.

They came flying up behind a coach that was trundling along the road.

The Ford Focus zipped out onto the other lane to overtake it.

Dropping down a gear, the Astra's two-litre engine roared and Nick felt himself pushed back into his seat as they topped 90 mph.

He felt frustrated that he hadn't heard back from dispatch yet. He grabbed the radio. 'Dispatch from three six. We are still in pursuit of suspect. Heading south on the A470, two miles north of Beaumaris. ETA of backup please, over.'

'Three six receiving. We have unit Bravo seven nine heading north on the A470, over,' the CAD informed him. 'ETA at your location, five minutes, over.'

'Received. Advise Bravo seven nine that we are in a high-speed pursuit of target vehicle and to proceed with caution, over,' Nick advised the CAD. He wanted Kevin Ball alive and at the speed they were travelling, it was getting incredibly dangerous.

Nick felt the Astra's rear tyres losing grip as they cornered another bend. His stomach lurched. They were still around twenty yards behind the car.

They came hammering up a hill and pulled out to overtake a caravan. It went past in a blur. Suddenly, a motorbike pulled out in front of them and they swerved to avoid it.

'For fuck's sake!' French hissed as he straightened the car.

They were now about ten yards behind Ball.

'Careful,' Nick said. 'I don't want to be pulling him dead out of the car.'

Without warning, the Ford Focus suddenly slowed and veered across the road. French hit the brakes to avoid clipping the back of the car.

Nick watched in frustration as Ball's car sped into a field.

'Bloody hell!' he said.

French spun the steering wheel and the back of the Astra skidded. For a heart-stopping moment, Nick thought they'd lost control of the car, but French spun the steering wheel the other way to straighten it as they drove into the field in pursuit.

The Ford Focus left a trail of dirt and dust as it zipped diagonally across the freshly ploughed soil.

Hitting bumps and dips, Nick and French were thrown around inside the car as they continued the chase.

Looking up, Nick saw the car reach the other side of the field and head downhill into a wooded area.

It then disappeared out of sight.

'Bollocks!' he growled.

Turning right, they skidded off the field and onto the dirt track that led down into the dark woods.

The Ford Focus was nowhere to be seen.

As they slowed, Nick spotted that the track split off in three directions.

'Are you fucking joking?' he snarled.

There was no way of knowing where Ball had gone.

French slowed the car to a stop and wound down the windows in the hope that they might hear something that might indicate where he had gone.

Nothing.

Nick gave a frustrated sigh.

CHAPTER 51

Crystal Palace, London SE19

Eight p.m., 5 November 2013

Ruth sat nervously in the first floor flat she shared with her partner Sarah. Taking a deep breath, she took a long swig of white wine and then got up and went to the window as she had done every few minutes for the past two hours. She gazed down the dark residential street, searching, hoping, praying to see Sarah making her way back home.

There was no sight of her so Ruth went back to the sofa, drank more wine and took another cigarette from the packet. She lit it, took a long deep drag and blew a plume of smoke up into the air. She watched it as it settled and hung close to the white Victorian plaster ceiling rose.

The sky outside suddenly exploded with a series of loud bangs as colourful fireworks painted the darkness in red, silver and gold. The noise made Ruth flinch. She took another gulp of wine and another drag on her cigarette.

Sarah had left the flat just before eight a.m. as she did every day. Ruth knew her routine. Sarah would then get the 8:05 a.m. train to Victoria from Crystal Palace station and then make the five-minute walk to a medical centre where she worked as an occupational health nurse. She would then get the 5:34 p.m. train home and be back before six p.m.

However, Sarah had never arrived at work that morning. Ruth had received a phone call from her boss, Michael, at ten a.m. to ask if Sarah was all right. Not only had she not arrived at work, she hadn't called or messaged. It was completely out of character. Ruth had spent the rest of the day calling Sarah's phone but there was no reply. Again, it was so out of character. And then when she failed to arrive home, Ruth's anxiety had gone through the roof, and she had called someone she knew at the Missing Persons Unit at the South Area Borough Command.

She had then called her daughter Ella who lived in a flat share in Tooting.

The buzzer rang.

Looking down, she saw Ella standing on the doorstep. She buzzed her in and then heard Ella's feet clumping up the stairs.

Going to the door, Ruth looked at Ella and then burst into tears.

'Oh Mum,' Ella said, taking her in her arms.

'I'm so scared,' Ruth admitted as they came into the living room.

'I don't understand,' Ella said with a frown.

'Something is terribly wrong. She left to get her train, but she never got to work. She hasn't answered her phone all day. And she hasn't come home,' Ruth gabbled anxiously.

'Right,' Ella said, and then gestured to the sofa. 'Come on, let's sit down. There's got to be a logical explanation for this.'

'There isn't,' Ruth said, shaking her head. 'There really isn't. You know what Sarah's like about her work. She's conscientious. There is no way she just wouldn't turn up for work without calling. I keep going through it in my head.'

'Could she have arranged to meet someone for the day and just forgotten to tell work?' Ella suggested.

'No,' Ruth insisted. 'She wouldn't do that. And that would mean she hadn't told me.'

Ella made a face.

'Oh, you think she was having an affair?' Ruth asked angrily.

'No, of course not,' Ella said. 'I'm just thinking out loud, Mum.'

Ruth looked at her daughter. 'She wasn't having an affair.' Then Ruth thought for a second. 'And if she was, she was smart enough to have covered her tracks. She wouldn't just not turn up to work and not contact me so she could run off for the day with someone else. That doesn't make any sense.'

'I know,' Ella agreed, 'but it's just the sort of thing the police are going to ask, that's all.'

Ruth gave her a withering look. 'Thanks for that. I am aware of what the Missing Persons Unit are going to ask me.'

'Has she taken any clothes, makeup?'

'No. Nothing,' Ruth replied. 'She just had the stuff that she goes to work in every day.'

'Right.' Ella's face dropped.

There were a few seconds of silence.

Ruth's eyes filled with tears. 'What are we going to do? She's just vanished.'

CHAPTER 52

Nick and French sped into the town of Bethesda on the Bangor Road. Bethesda was on the western most edge of Snowdonia and about six miles south of the North Wales coastline. Garrow had done an electoral role search on the way and found the address of Ball's mother, Patricia.

Five minutes later, they pulled up outside a small white bungalow with a blue front door and matching garden gates. The front garden was full of potted plants that had been neatly arranged around the paving stones and on the stone wall that flanked the road. A hanging basket beside the front door, overflowing with yellow and purple violas, rocked back and forth in the strong wind. The idyllic scene looked as if it had come from a picture book.

Getting out of the car, Nick pulled up his collar against the wind as he and French marched up the garden path. Nick gave an authoritative knock on the door and took a step back.

A few seconds later, a cheery woman in her sixties opened the door. She had a ruddy face and thinning silver hair. She wore an old-fashioned primrose-coloured twinset and a long skirt. She dressed older than her actual age, Nick thought to himself.

'DS Evans and DS French, Llancastell CID,' Nick said politely, showing her his warrant card. 'We're looking for a Patricia Ball?'

'Yes,' she said, now looking concerned.

'You're Patricia Ball?' Nick asked to confirm.

'Yes, that's right,' she said with a furrowed brow. 'Whatever is the matter?'

Nick gestured to inside the cottage. 'Is it okay if we come in for a moment? It's just a couple of routine questions.'

She nodded uncertainly and opened the door fully. 'Erm, yes okay.'

They went through and into a small dark hallway. There were a few coats and two black umbrellas hanging up beside an old-fashioned mirror. The air smelled of stewed tea and musty old books.

'Do you want to come and sit down for a minute?' she asked apprehensively.

'Yes, thank you,' French replied.

The living room was old-fashioned but neat and tidy. The walls were covered with cream wallpaper with a dark green floral pattern. There were shelves filled with paperback books and a table that had several family photos in a line.

Nick took a surreptitious glance at the photos. One of them featured a couple with two children. Nick assumed that the young boy in the photo was Kevin Ball. From the look of the photo, Patricia and her husband had had their children later in life. At the far end of the table there was a more recent photo of Ball in his late twenties. If he had to guess, Nick thought it could only be a year or two old.

Sitting down on the sofa, Nick and French watched Patricia as she lowered herself into an armchair. She seemed to wince as she sat down.

'Sorry,' she said as she blew out her cheeks and then settled in her chair. 'Terrible arthritis in my knees. Comes and goes, thankfully.'

'We're looking for Kevin, Mrs Ball,' Nick explained in an innocuous tone.

'Patricia, please.'

French pulled out a notepad and pen. 'Have you seen him?'

'No,' she said, shaking her head. Then she immediately scratched her face.

She's lying, Nick thought instantly. The scratch was a *tell*.

Over on the coffee table, there were two mugs and two side plates. Someone had been here very recently.

French smiled kindly at her. 'Could you tell us when you last saw your son?'

She sighed. 'I'm afraid it's been a very long time. We had a falling out many years ago.'

'Right,' Nick said with a thoughtful expression. 'When you say a very long time…'

'I haven't seen Kevin since his twenty-first birthday,' Patricia explained. 'He went off the rails. It makes me very sad when I think about it.'

Well, you've got a photo of him on your table and he's definitely in his late twenties, so I know you're lying.

'Would your husband have had any contact with him?' French asked.

'I'm afraid he passed two years ago,' she said quietly.

'I'm sorry to hear that.'

Nick pulled out one of his contact cards and handed it to her. 'If Kevin does decide to get in contact with you, can you tell him that we'd like to speak to him?'

'Of course,' Patricia replied. 'But I don't think he will. I'm not surprised that he's in trouble again.'

Nick and French got up from the sofa and headed out to the hall.

'Oh, I didn't even offer you a cup of tea,' she said, shaking her head as she pushed herself out of the armchair.

'That's fine. Don't get up. We'll see ourselves out,' Nick reassured her as his eyes gazed around the hall and the table. There was a black car key lying loose with a tiny, green marijuana leaf attached as the key ring.

Yeah, I'm pretty sure that's not your car key, Nick thought suspiciously. However, he was going to leave and let her believe that she'd got away with it.

'Thanks for your help,' he said with a forced smile as they left.

'Goodbye now,' Patricia said, as she hobbled behind them and closed the door.

Nick waited a moment halfway down the garden path.

'Kevin has definitely been there,' he said under his breath as he scoured the area.

'Yeah, I clocked the two mugs and two plates on the coffee table,' French stated.

'Plus the car key with a marijuana leaf on the hall table,' Nick added.

French gave him a wry smile. 'Which I didn't spot.'

To the right of the bungalow, Nick noticed a separate garage. 'Come on, I've got a very strong feeling that there's going to be a white Ford Focus in there.'

They got to the garage and tried the wooden doors, but they were locked.

Moving around the side, Nick spied a side door with a small, dirty glass panel.

He cupped his hand against the panel and squinted.

Bingo!

The white Ford Focus was sitting inside the garage.

'The car's in here,' Nick said to French, and then gestured back to the front door. 'Time for another word with the lovely Patricia.'

Banging on the door, Nick took a step back and could feel his annoyance rising.

Patricia opened the door and gave them a confused, innocent expression. 'Sorry, I...'

'Patricia Ball, I'm arresting you for obstruction and aiding and abetting an offender under Section 44 of the Serious Crime Act,' Nick growled at her.

'What? But I...' Patricia stammered.

'Not interested,' Nick snapped. 'So, unless you want to go to prison, I'm going to need the make, model and registration of the car that Kevin is now driving.'

'I've no idea what you're talking about,' she snivelled.

Nick looked at French. 'Cuff her.'

French took her arm.

'He didn't mean to do it,' she sobbed. 'It was an accident.'

'Where is Kevin going?' Nick thundered.

'I don't know. I swear to you,' she mumbled. 'He said he just lost his temper and...'

Nick held out his hand. 'I'm going to need your phone, right now,' he said forcefully.

Patricia blinked and wiped away a tear. 'I don't have a phone,' she whimpered. But her eyes betrayed her as she glanced nervously in the living room.

'Thanks,' Nick said caustically. 'See if you can find a logbook anywhere Dan.'

Nick moved quickly across the hallway and into the living room. There was a mobile phone sitting on the armchair. He assumed that Patricia had called or was about to call Kevin to inform him of their visit.

Grabbing the phone, he saw that the lock screen hadn't yet been activated and that the screen was still open. He scrolled through and found his way to the phone's text messages.

There was a text from Kevin from twenty minutes earlier.

> Thanks for coming to my rescue, Mum. You've always been there for me. I'll ring once I get to Ireland. Weather forecast isn't good which is a bit scary as you know I don't like being on boats at the best of times. Think I was sick the last time I was on a ferry! LOL. Love Kev xx

French burst into the room and waved a logbook. 'Renault Megane. Silver. The reg is in here.'

'Great,' Nick said, as he gestured to the phone. 'Ball is getting a ferry to Ireland. I assume he's going to Holyhead.'

CHAPTER 53

It was forty minutes later by the time Nick and French arrived at Holyhead, where the ferries travelled over to Dublin. Nick had put out a request for all units to be on the lookout for Patricia's Renault Megane, but so far they'd drawn a blank. The rain had stopped and the black clouds seemed to have retreated to the east.

Pulling into the enormous Holyhead Port, they scoured the area to see if they could see Ball or the car. There were cars and lorries everywhere. They were essentially looking for a needle in a haystack.

Getting out of the car, Nick looked over at a spindly security guard who was wearing a green hi vis vest and carrying a clipboard.

'Afternoon. We're over from the mainland. Llancastell CID,' Nick said as he pulled out his warrant card.

'Christ! You've come a long way. Must be serious,' the security guard chortled.

'Yeah, it is. It's a murder case,' Nick replied in a tone to demonstrate that it wasn't actually that funny.

The man pulled an embarrassed face.

French stared at him. 'We need to know when the next ferry leaves for Dublin?'

The guard, who now looked a little sheepish, pointed further along the port side. 'That's the next one there. She doesn't go for another hour though.'

'If I was trying to avoid detection, where would be the best place to hide in plain sight?' Nick asked.

The guard pointed to an extensive building down on the right. 'The terminal centre down there has got fast food places, coffee shops, bookshops and toilets. It's pretty busy so I'd try there.'

'Thanks.' Nick and French made their way past the articulated lorries that waited in vast lines for docks marked *Freight*. The air was thick with diesel fumes and a hint of the Irish Sea. Gulls swooped and cawed incessantly.

They got to the terminal centre. Chairs and tables were spread out in little groupings outside each shop, and the entire area was busy with passengers walking to and fro. People were walking their dogs, smoking in little groups or eating takeaway food.

For the next ten minutes, Nick and French spread out to opposite sides of the concourse and scoured every shop and seating area. Eventually, they met back at the far end.

'Nothing,' Nick sighed in frustration.

'Maybe we got it wrong,' French suggested.

'Yeah, we haven't factored in that he might have gone across to Liverpool to get a ferry.'

There were a few seconds as Nick tried to think what to do next. They could feed the Megane's registration into the automatic number plate recognition – ANPR – computer system across North Wales. But that would take hours, if not a whole day. And by then Ball could be in Ireland and therefore very difficult to find.

Out of the corner of his eye, Nick spotted a man leaning with his back against a wall beside a coffee bar. For a moment, he didn't notice anything more than the black baseball cap.

A baseball cap that had distinctive green writing that he'd seen before.

As the man turned, Nick saw his face.

Kevin Ball.

'Over there,' Nick said under his breath, pointing.

French raised an eyebrow. 'Where am I looking?'

'Black baseball cap outside Costa,' Nick said as they started to move towards that area, being careful not to alert Ball to the fact that they'd seen him.

They moved swiftly, zig-zagging their way through queues of passengers and seated areas, eyes focused on Ball who was sipping his coffee, still unaware that he'd been spotted.

Suddenly, he looked their way. He frowned as he did a double take.

Dropping his coffee, he turned and sprinted away.

Shit! He's seen us.

'Bollocks,' French growled, and they took off after him.

Nick held up his warrant card as he and French weaved through the passengers.

'Out of the way! Police!' he yelled.

Ball knocked a man and woman flying as he ran across the concourse.

Nick sidestepped a young couple with a pram and nearly lost his footing.

'Sorry,' he muttered, now out of breath.

Up ahead, Ball glanced back for a second and then smashed through the green fire exit doors and threw them closed behind him.

A few seconds later, Nick and French crashed through the doors after him.

They were now at the back of the shopping centre. Huge steel bins were lined up against a tall, wire mesh fence. The air was thick with the smell of rubbish and the diesel fumes of the nearby articulated lorries.

To their right, there were three dark blue Portakabins, a JCB digger, cones and a cement mixer. However, there seemed to be no one around.

'Where the hell is he?' French said, trying to get his breath.

Nick glanced left and right, but Ball had disappeared.

Thinking that he saw some kind of movement from behind one of the Portakabins, Nick signalled to French that he thought Ball might be hiding there.

As they approached, a huge blue articulated lorry thundered past on the road beyond the fence to the back of the Portakabins. The smell of diesel fuel filled the air.

Nick indicated for French to go around the Portakabins to their left, while he would move round to the right in a pincer movement.

With his pulse still throbbing in his ear, Nick moved cautiously to the side of the cabin and then stopped. He took a deep breath as he strained his hearing for any sound of movement.

Nothing.

He can't have gone far.

With his back to the wooden side panel, Nick slowly glanced down the back of the cabin.

There were a couple of huge steel bins but Ball was nowhere to be seen.

Bollocks.

A lorry sounded its horn on the road behind them. It was so loud that its sound seemed to split the air and made Nick flinch for a second.

He glanced over at French, who was now creeping along slowly. They both signalled that they had seen nothing.

If Ball had come this way, the only place he could be hiding was behind the steel bins.

Nick made a jabbing signal towards the bins to indicate to French that he thought Ball was hiding there.

French nodded in agreement.

Taking a few cautious steps over the weed-strewn ground, Nick braced himself. He didn't want Ball to come out and attack them.

Holding his breath, he craned his head to see if he could see anything.

Suddenly, Ball jumped out.

'Stay back!' he shouted, as he brandished a two-foot length of wood that had nails sticking out of it.

Jesus!

'Woah!' Nick said, putting up his hands as he backed away.

'Put that down, Kevin!' French said calmly.

'Fuck off,' Ball yelled as he swung the wood at them.

Nick looked at him, making sure that he made eye contact. 'Kevin, you need to put that down. You're only going to make things much worse.'

'Worse? I'm not going to go to prison. No way,' he said, sounding desperate. 'I didn't mean to do it. I just snapped.'

'Okay,' Nick said gently. 'Why don't you put that down? Then we can go back to the station, have a cup of tea and you can tell us exactly what happened, eh?'

'Fuck that!' Ball shook his head. 'You know that bitch slept with Matty? Behind my back,' he sneered with gritted teeth. 'After all I've been through with her, and she does that to me!'

'I can see that you're angry. And that's understandable,' French said in a reassuring tone. 'But we can't help you while you're swinging that thing around.'

Ball nodded as if he understood what French had said. His whole demeanour changed. He looked defeated and broken.

French stepped forwards and gestured. 'Come on, Kev. Give me that and then we can sort all this out.'

'I don't think I can handle going to prison,' he muttered under his breath.

Nick relaxed for a second. It seemed that Ball had conceded that there was no way out of this but to hand himself in peacefully.

Suddenly, without warning, Ball swung the piece of wood at French.

French ducked out of the way but tripped and fell to the ground.

Ball ran towards Nick, who dived out of the way, narrowly avoiding the wood and the nails. He crashed to the ground, grazing his palms and his knees.

Throwing the piece of wood to one side, Ball sprinted for a gap in the mesh fence.

'Kevin!' Nick yelled as he tried to get to his feet.

Ducking through the fence, Ball ran full pelt across the uneven ground as he headed for the quayside.

Without looking, he ran into the road.

The air split with the sound of an articulated lorry's horn.

Ball stopped, looked left and froze.

Oh God!

Nick held his breath.

A 40-tonne lorry slammed on its brakes, but it was too late.

The lorry smashed into Ball and then he disappeared under it.

He was killed instantly.

CHAPTER 54

Four hours later, Nick was sitting opposite Superintendent Jones in his office on the top floor of Llancastell nick. It was getting dark and the rain had started to fall outside. The raindrops pattered onto the large glass window of Jones' office. The dotted lights of Llancastell stretched away into the distance before the shadowy ridges of Snowdonia loomed on the horizon.

Jones' office was large and tidy but impersonal. There were a couple of photos of him in his full police dress uniform receiving various police medals and commendations.

'It's a bit of a mess,' Jones said under his breath as he thumbed through Nick and French's initial report on the events at Holyhead and Ball's death. Jones was thickset and balding with a strong North Wales accent.

Nick knew how this was going to go. Jones was a political animal with his eye on the top job in the North Wales Police force. Therefore every decision he ever took was made with that in mind. Not only did that make him both cautious and indecisive, it also meant that his primary purpose was to cover his arse in every situation.

'What the hell happened over there?' he asked, as he looked again at Nick's report.

'Like it says in my report, sir,' Nick replied, 'Ball charged at us. He had a weapon. DS French and I got out of his way to protect ourselves. In doing this, we both ended up on the ground. And Ball ran across the road into the path of an oncoming lorry. He didn't stand a chance.'

Jones held up a printout. 'There's an eyewitness who claims that you and DS French were chasing the suspect when he ran in front of the lorry.'

'No, sir,' Nick said adamantly as he shook his head. 'That is not correct. That's not what happened and I stand by what is in mine and DS French's version of events.'

'Okay. But the press are having a field day over this,' Jones explained. 'Social media are all over it, accusing North Wales Police of being responsible for his death.'

'Like I said, it was Ball's decision to run into the path of that lorry,' Nick said calmly, even though the thought of what was on social media was making him increasingly anxious. 'He wasn't cornered and we didn't chase him.'

'Obviously I've got your back on this, Nick,' Jones said. 'I just don't want to be handed some CCTV from Holyhead showing me anything other than what's in both of your reports.'

'That's not going to happen, sir,' Nick reassured him.

'I know that,' Jones said, giving him a supportive nod. 'Just make sure all the paperwork on this investigation is watertight. Because the IOPC are going to be all over it and you know what they're like.'

The IOPC stood for The Independent Office for Police Conduct who were responsible for overseeing any serious complaints made against police forces in England or Wales. Essentially, they were the internal affairs department who had the power to initiate their own investigations without relying on a particular force to make a referral.

Nick nodded. Officers from the IOPC were renowned for being at best pedantic, and at worst hostile and arrogant.

'And you've spoken to your rep?' Jones asked.

'Yeah,' Nick replied. 'We're meeting tomorrow.'

Jones was referring to Nick's representative from the Police Federation, which was the closest thing the police force had to a trade union.

'Good, good. You're going to be fine, Nick,' Jones said as he got up from his desk, which was a signal that their meeting was now over.

He came over and gave Nick a firm handshake, pressing his thumb over Nick's first and second knuckles. It was the Masonic secret handshake which Nick had felt before. But Nick had no time for masons or their secret ceremonies.

'Thank you, sir,' he said as he turned and headed for the door.

CHAPTER 55

Nick took a step into the empty lift on the ground floor of the Llancastell University Hospital. He blew out his cheeks. It had been a very challenging day. The aftermath of the accident at Holyhead in which Kevin Ball had been killed had been extremely stressful. He was still anxious about the IOPC investigation into the incident, but his Police Federation rep had told him not to worry.

Nick watched the metallic doors of the lift clunk shut and felt the slight shift as the lift went up. He had only been back on duty as a CID detective for a matter of weeks. Even though he understood the important role that the IOPC did in rooting out police corruption, he couldn't help resenting them scrutinising what had happened at Holyhead that day. There was no way that a member of the public had seen him and Dan chasing Ball into the road because it just hadn't happened. Unfortunately that was the way of the world these days. Some people were just looking for police officers to make a mistake before hammering them publicly.

The lift doors opened and Nick's mind now turned to Ruth. Even though he knew that he needed to support Sarah and Ella at her bedside, it had been incredibly difficult to watch Ruth react and talk like someone else. She had been unrecognisable.

Arriving at the ICU, Nick gave the ward sister a smile as he headed down the empty corridor towards Ruth's room. Ella was standing outside with her mobile phone held to her ear. She ended the call and popped the phone back in her pocket before looking up and seeing Nick approaching.

'Hey,' he said as he gave her a hug.

'Hi Nick,' Ella said, sounding weary.

'Any change?' he asked hopefully.

She shook her head sadly. 'No. Mum's being her usual delightful self,' she said, trying to force a smile.

'It's going to change,' Nick said, trying to allay her fears. 'She is going to get better.'

Ella nodded unconvincingly as he went to the door and opened it.

Ruth was lying asleep in the bed and Sarah was sleeping in a padded chair in the corner of the room.

'Maybe I should come back?' Nick suggested. 'If everyone's sleeping.'

There was part of Nick that just wanted to avoid seeing Ruth the way she was, especially after the day he'd had.

'No, it's fine,' Ella said quietly. 'You never know, it might be your voice that Mum responds to.'

Nick nodded but he wasn't convinced.

Just do the right thing, mate, he told himself.

He took off his coat and went and sat on the chair on the far side of the bed.

For a few seconds, he looked over at Ruth, over-whelmed by a feeling of sadness and loss.

'Hi, Ruth,' he said quietly. 'It's Nick here. I've just come straight from work actually. To say I've had a chal-lenging day doesn't really do it justice. After all, it's not every day that you watch a suspect run in front of a

40-tonne articulated lorry and get squashed. Of course, there's some twatty member of the great British public who reckons they saw me and Dan chase that suspect into the road. So, as you can imagine, the world and his wife have now got a bloody opinion on that one. We've got the IOPC sniffing around. Jones is doing exactly what you'd expect him to and trying to cover his arse and…'

'What the bloody hell are you rattling on about?' said a voice.

It was Ruth.

She looked at him through a half-opened eye.

Nick's heart sank. He prepared himself for Ruth not recognising him and being abusive and irritable.

'Sorry, I…' Nick said gently as he looked over at Ella. She looked equally demoralised.

'Hi Ruth,' he said cautiously. 'I was just filling you in on my day.'

'I'm well aware of that,' Ruth said.

'Sorry, I…' Nick wasn't sure what to say next.

Ella glanced over and gave him a sympathetic look.

'If you've got the IOPC sniffing around, I hope you've spoken to your police rep at least,' Ruth said in a calm voice.

What did she say?

Nick did a double take and then looked over at Ella who was already standing with a surprised look on her face.

'Mum?' she said hesitantly.

Did she just say what I think she said?

Ruth turned her head to look at Ella. She frowned and there was a terrible silence for a few seconds.

'Mum?' Ella's tone was cautious, even frightened.

'Hello, darling,' Ruth said. Her voice was croaky. 'Have you been here the whole time?'

Nick stood up in amazement.

'Oh my God, Mum,' Ella cried, her eyes filling with tears.

'It's okay,' Ruth said as she opened her eyes fully. 'I'm okay. Well, I feel like shit, and my mouth feels like sandpaper but I'm okay...'

Ella went over to the jug of water and poured some into the beaker. Her hands were shaking with emotion.

'Here you go, Mum,' she sighed.

'Your hands are shaking,' Ruth said.

'We thought we'd lost you,' Ella tried to explain as she handed her the water and put her hand on her mother's shoulder.

'Don't worry, I'm not going anywhere quite yet,' Ruth said as she coughed and then took a sip of water.

'Sarah's here,' Ella said, pointing over to the chair where Sarah was starting to stir.

'Is she?' Ruth said, trying to sit up.

'Hey, be careful,' Nick said as he took her arm and moved her pillows.

'Sarah,' Ella called over. 'It's Mum. She's... well, she's back...'

Sarah frowned and looked very confused. 'I don't understand.'

'Hello, buster,' Ruth croaked.

'Bloody hell, aren't you a sight for sore eyes?' Sarah said, leaping up, going to the bed and hugging her.

'Ow, ow, careful,' Ruth said with a wince. 'Remember I've been shot.'

'Sorry,' Sarah said, moving back and wiping a tear from her face. 'That was a few days ago.'

'Was it?' Ruth asked with a furrowed brow. 'How long was I out?'

'Nearly four days,' Ella said. 'They put you into an induced coma. And then when you did come round, it was like that scene from *The Exorcist*.'

'I'm so confused,' Ruth said. 'What are you talking about?'

'Well, you seemed conscious,' Nick explained, 'but you didn't recognise us and you were vile. And then your head started spinning around and...'

'Oh fuck off,' Ruth laughed.

Sarah sat on the side of the bed. 'You scared the shit out of us.'

Ruth pulled a face. 'Sorry. I'll try not to get shot again.' Then she looked at them all. 'Do you know what I really fancy?'

'A cup of tea?' Sarah suggested.

'No. A huge glass of wine and a ciggie,' Ruth said with a grin.

Nick looked at Ella and Sarah. 'Yeah, she's definitely back.'

CHAPTER 56

It was the following morning and Nick had an extra spring in his step. Seeing Ruth back to her old self was incredible. He had been able to go home and tell Megan that her Auntie Ruth was feeling better and she could see her very soon.

Sitting at Ruth's desk no longer felt so upsetting. Sarah had called later in the evening to say that the doctors were confident that Ruth would eventually return to full health – if she convalesced properly. She might even be able to leave hospital towards the end of the week to recuperate at home.

Grabbing his coffee, Nick went out into the CID office which was now buzzing with chatter. The news that Ruth was officially on the road to recovery had given everyone a huge boost.

'Morning everyone,' Nick said as he put his coffee down on the table. 'I'm guessing that by now all of you know the good news about the boss. I saw her last night and for the first time she seemed recognisable as her old self. In fact, she said she wanted a glass of wine and a ciggie, so she was definitely feeling better.'

There was laughter from some of the assembled team.

'Any idea how long before we're going to see her back at work?' Garrow asked.

'No, sorry Jim,' Nick admitted. 'Due to the gunshot wound and her cardiac arrest, it's going to be months rather than weeks. But the main thing is that she's out of danger and, so far, there are no signs that she sustained any serious brain damage.' Nick looked out at them all and smiled. 'It really is such good news.'

There were some murmurs of agreement from the room.

Letting out an audible sigh, Nick perched on the table and then looked over at the scene board. 'However, we do have to tie up the loose ends of this case. As most of you know, Kevin Ball died in an accident at Holyhead ferry terminal yesterday. Dan and I had pursued him there. We followed him from the shopping centre. He was armed with a makeshift weapon. Having tried to persuade him to put the weapon down, he charged at us and then made a run for the quayside. Unfortunately, he ran into the path of an oncoming lorry and was killed instantly.' Nick frowned for a moment. 'I know that the news and social media are suggesting that Dan and I chased Kevin into the road and so we are somehow responsible for his death. But that's just not what happened. Obviously, the IOPC will be holding a full enquiry into the incident. And they will require access to all our files relating to this investigation.'

There was a collective groan. The IOPC were *persona non grata* amongst a lot of the rank and file of the police force.

'So, please, please, make sure every "i" is dotted, every "t" is crossed,' Nick said in a serious tone. 'I do not want to give them any excuse to come in here and tear this place apart. Triple check your witness statements. Same with our requests for phone records, bank statements, CCTV, ANPR, everything… Dan?'

French cleared his throat as he got up and made his way over to the scene board. He pointed to a photo. 'I know that up until yesterday, Layla Hughes had been our prime suspect for Matty Hopkins' murder. And of course that was a legitimate line of enquiry. We had several witness statements that showed that Layla had become obsessed with Matty. She had begun to stalk him at the holiday park. She attacked another woman who had slept with him, resulting in her being sacked. And, on the night that Matty was murdered, she admitted to drugging him with GHB to get him to stay over at her flat. When Matty left, she followed him towards the Pen-y-Bryn Holiday Park.' French then pointed to the printout of a map that had been pinned to the scene board. 'However, a trace of the GPS of Layla's mobile phone revealed her exact movements on Saturday night. And the trace showed that she followed Matty for about five hundred yards up to these woods, before turning around and heading back to her flat for the rest of the evening and the following morning until she started work at the café.'

'Thanks Dan,' Nick said as he went over to the board again. 'Just to bring you all up to speed, the case against Kevin Ball started to escalate yesterday. We already knew that he had been at the fire at the cabin. He had burns to the palms of his hands which he claimed had been caused when he tried to put out the fire in his car. He then lied about his whereabouts and disappeared for the rest of Saturday night. However, until yesterday we had no concrete motive. But then we found photographs of Matty and Kat Mount, Kevin's girlfriend, having sex. Kat admitted that Kevin had found out about her and Matty sleeping together. That explains Miles Hopkins' account of having to pull Matty and Kevin apart during an altercation. Our theory is that on Saturday night Kevin spotted Matty returning to the holiday park, clearly very unsteady from drinking and having his drink spiked with GHB. He then followed Matty and watched as he went inside the vacant cabin to sleep it off. He took the keys out of the door and locked Matty inside. He went over to the maintenance shed where he grabbed two cans of petrol which he then used to burn down the cabin with Matty inside.'

'What about the CCTV we have from the park?' Garrow asked.

Georgie looked over. 'It's going to take a few more days to get that back from Manchester.'

French looked over. 'Kevin admitted his guilt to us yesterday. So the IOPC can do their worst but I'm clear that he was guilty of Matty's murder and that his death was an accident of his own making.'

There were murmurs of agreement from the team.

'Right, guys. We have plenty of work to be getting on with,' Nick said in a positive tone. 'Let's get all this checked over. I'll be in the DI's office if anyone needs me.'

CHAPTER 57

Five days later

It was late morning and Nick and Georgie arrived at St Joseph's Church in Colwyn Bay. They had gone to represent the North Wales Police force at a memorial service for Matty Hopkins. His funeral was due the following week but was restricted to family only.

Nick and Georgie walked carefully across the graveyard to the church entrance. The spring air smelled sweet and aromatic. The graveyard was weathered with pale grey tombs that gradually melted into the light. As he manoeuvred between the graves, Nick's shoes crunched noisily against the winding gravel pathway. Dark green moss had grown over many of the older headstones, obscuring their shapes and sizes. The lettering had faded from time and weather. Up ahead stood a monument resembling an altar, with clearly deep-engraved rows of names. Its granite face had seaweed-like tufts of lichen poking out from its seams.

Turning towards the church, Nick spotted various mourners who were huddled and talking in low voices. He recognised various people who worked at the holiday park.

Out of the corner of his eye, he spotted a figure standing behind a large gravestone about fifty yards away.

It was Layla Hughes. When she saw him, she just glared in his direction. He didn't blame her. He had accused her of Matty's murder. Unfortunately that was part of the investigation process. The fact that she had stalked and drugged Matty did mean that his suspicions were well grounded.

'If looks could kill,' Georgie said under her breath as she spotted Layla looking at them.

'I'm sure she'll get over it,' Nick replied.

'My money was definitely on her,' Georgie admitted.

'Me too,' Nick agreed. 'And at the risk of speaking ill of the dead, Matty Hopkins was pretty reckless with other people's feelings.'

Georgie gave him a quizzical look. 'You think he deserved what happened to him?'

'God no,' Nick replied. 'I guess he just wasn't entirely innocent in all this.' He then gestured towards the main church doors. 'Shall we go in?'

'Yes,' Georgie said.

Miles Hopkins was standing close to the doors, greeting those who had come to mourn his son. He was handing out an order of service with a photograph of Matty on the front.

He looked up and saw them approaching.

'Thank you for coming,' he said quietly as he reached out and shook their hands.

'Of course,' Nick said quietly.

There was an awkward silence as he handed them both an order of service.

Miles looked at them. 'I don't think there's anything worse than having to bury your child. And we've had to do this twice.'

Nick gave him an empathetic nod. 'I can't imagine how difficult this must be for you… Is Jane here?'

'Yes,' Miles said, and he gestured over to a figure in the distance who was crouched down by a grave with some flowers. 'Jane likes to have a little chat with her daughter Sophie whenever we come here.'

'Of course,' Georgie said gently.

'And thank you for finding out what happened to Matty,' Miles said with a sad expression. 'It does help a little for us to know who…' He was lost in emotion for a second. 'You know? But I'm not glad that Kevin was killed. His death isn't going to bring Matty back. I know some people might think differently and think that he deserved that. But Jane and I aren't like that.'

Nick gave him an understanding nod as he and Georgie went inside the church.

Glancing back over into the graveyard, he saw that Layla Hughes had gone.

–

Forty minutes later, Nick and Georgie started to make their way out of the church with the song *The Masterplan* by Oasis playing quietly. It had been said during the service that Oasis was Matty's favourite band. There had been some moving tributes from old friends and from Miles Hopkins.

Nick had recognised that it wasn't until he had heard others talking about Matty that he had a clear idea of what he was like as a young man. That was the curious thing about many investigations like this one. You wouldn't know the victim and had to rely on the testimony of others who did. Nick had to admit that, for what it was worth, his impression of Matty had softened during the service.

As Nick and Georgie left, he saw Jane Hopkins approaching them.

'Hi there,' she said. Her eyes were puffy from where she had been crying. 'I know my husband has already spoken to you, but I wanted to thank you personally. I was so worried that you wouldn't be able to find the person who set fire to the cabin.'

'It's not really how we wanted this to turn out,' Nick admitted. 'Ideally I would have liked to have seen Kevin Ball stand trial for what he did.'

'Of course. And so would Miles and I,' Jane said thoughtfully. 'But I think knowing who was responsible does help a little. Please pass on my thanks to everyone who worked on the investigation.'

Georgie gave her a kind smile. 'We will do.'

Nick and Georgie turned and began to walk back along the gravel pathway though the graveyard. The day was now warm and there was no more than a light breeze. There were birds chattering tunefully in the trees above them.

As they neared the grave where Nick had spotted Jane laying flowers, he stopped to have a respectful look.

There was a small white headstone with pink roses embossed in the top right-hand corner. It read:

Precious Memories of
Our Dear Daughter
SOPHIE CHARLOTTE HOPKINS
April 22 2011
June 1 2017

For a few seconds, Nick and Georgie looked at the grave reflectively. Nick couldn't help but think of Megan. He couldn't imagine the pain of losing her. It would be unbearable.

Georgie frowned. She was deep in thought.

'You okay?' Nick asked, assuming that she was moved by being at the grave.

'It's so terribly sad,' Georgie said. But then she looked at him. 'The 1 of June 2017?'

Nick didn't know what she was talking about. 'Sorry, you've lost me,' he admitted.

'The date,' Georgie said. 'I've seen it somewhere before.'

'Okay,' Nick said, still none the wiser.

'Sorry, I'm not being very clear.'

'No.'

'I mean I've seen that date written down somewhere very recently,' she explained with a furrowed brow. 'In some kind of official document. Don't ask where, but it rings a bell.'

Nick looked at her. He had no idea what the relevance would be, and as far as CID were concerned, the case was virtually closed.

CHAPTER 58

Ruth moved around so that her legs swung off the side of the hospital bed. She'd been transferred to a general ward from ICU two days ago, and after a lot of pushing and cajoling, the doctors had been persuaded to allow her to go home. Given the noise on the general ward, Ruth was pretty sure that she would get more rest and peace and quiet at home. Sarah had assured the ward sister that Ruth would be well looked after.

Taking a deep breath, Ruth winced for a moment. She was still taking strong painkillers for the gunshot wound and once in a while she got a sharp stabbing pain in her stomach. The doctor had assured her that this was normal and part of the healing process.

Looking around, she saw Helga, a German woman in her fifties, whom Ruth had had several conversations with in the past two days. Helga gave a little wave. She was recovering from heart surgery but expected to make a full recovery.

'Remember to come and visit, Ruth,' she said in her strong German accent.

Helga ran a café in Llanberis and Ruth had promised to pop in the next time she was nearby.

'Of course. I'm looking forward to it. Apple strudel is literally my favourite pudding in the world.'

Helga gave a little laugh.

Ruth moved her feet onto the floor and slipped on the shoes that Sarah had brought her from home. They didn't really match the navy trackie bottoms she was wearing but she didn't care. She was going home. And she was alive.

It had only dawned on her since moving to the general ward how close she had come to losing her life. While she'd been in the coma, it felt like her whole life had flashed in front of her. Snippets of memories. Tiny snatches of conversations or songs. Maybe that had all added to her feeling of gratitude, perspective and a different way of looking at life.

'Here we go,' Sarah said quietly as she came into the ward and approached with a wheelchair.

'Can I just make it clear, I'm not happy about being pushed out of here in that thing,' Ruth groaned.

'You were shot and you nearly died,' Sarah said, rolling her eyes. 'It's okay for you to be in a wheelchair.'

Ruth smiled at her. 'I know.' She got to her feet but felt a little dizzy. 'Yeah, okay, the wheelchair is a good idea actually.'

'Feeling dizzy?' Sarah asked knowingly.

'Yep,' Ruth said as she lowered herself into the red padded seat.

'Well sit down in this you fool.'

'Charming.'

'The doctor said you're going to have dizzy spells for a while,' Sarah said as she turned the wheelchair around.

Ruth gave Helga a wave, along with a couple of the other women, as they left the ward and went down towards the lifts.

'Actually, I could get quite used to this,' Ruth joked. 'Home James and...'

'...don't spare the horses,' Sarah said, rolling her eyes again.

'God, I must be getting predictable.'

'Don't joke about me pushing you in a wheelchair,' Sarah laughed. 'You're older than me so this might be a preview of our life in thirty years.'

'Don't remind me,' Ruth groaned as the lift doors opened.

Sarah pushed her inside. 'Here we go.'

The doors to the lift closed with a metallic clunk.

'Ground floor, perfumery, stationery and leather goods, wigs and haberdashery, kitchenware and food, going up,' Ruth sang. It was the theme tune to a 70s sit com, *Are You Being Served?*.

'You seem very chipper?'

'I am.' Ruth turned her head to look up at Sarah. 'Actually, I've been doing some thinking.'

'Yeah, I'm pretty sure the doctor told you not to do that,' Sarah quipped.

'Ha ha. I'm being serious,' Ruth said. 'I think I'm going to retire.'

Sarah's eyes widened. 'What?'

'Seriously. I can get my pension early. Spend more time with you and Daniel. Help you look after your mum.'

Sarah frowned. 'But you love your job?'

'And I just got shot and nearly died,' Ruth replied. 'I've spent nearly thirty years as a police officer. I think I've earned the right to take things a little easier.'

'Hey, I'm not going to stand in your way, if that's what you really want to do,' Sarah said, and then she raised an eyebrow. 'There is, of course, a big problem with you being retired.'

'What's that?'

'I'd have to spend more time with you,' she joked. 'You'd be getting under my feet. And getting on my nerves.'

'Very funny,' Ruth chuckled.

'Do you mean right away?' Sarah asked.

'Given my injury, I'm pretty sure it would just be a question of filling out the paperwork.'

'Great,' Sarah said with a beaming smile. She leaned down and kissed Ruth on the mouth. 'That's really great.'

CHAPTER 59

It was nine a.m. and Georgie was queuing up in the canteen to get a cup of decaffeinated coffee and some toast. She felt a little flutter in her tummy. There were still moments when she would forget that she was pregnant. And then something would remind her, and she would get the surreal thought that another human being was growing inside her. And that would blow her mind for a few seconds.

Now that she'd had a few weeks to get used to the idea, the anxiety seemed to have abated for the most part. Sometimes she was incredibly excited. But there were also times, usually at four a.m., when she wondered what the hell she was doing. How was she going to cope on her own? Even though Pam and Bill had reassured her that they would be there every step of the way, it wasn't quite the same as having a husband or partner to share the highs and lows of pregnancy with and then bring a new baby home. And in those moments, Georgie would feel terribly alone and scared.

'You look miles away,' said a voice behind her.

It was Nick. He gave her a friendly smile.

'Yeah, I was,' she admitted.

He gave her a supportive look. 'You feeling okay? You know, being back at work? You're still owed convalescence time, so if you need some time at home… Especially as we're only tying up the loose ends of the case now?'

Oh, he's so lovely, she thought.

She reached over and touched his arm. 'I'm fine. Thank you. If I stay at home I'll just read articles telling me that I can't eat goats' cheese, Brie or Camembert. And that I can't have any caffeine.'

Nick pointed to her coffee with a quizzical look.

'Don't worry, it's decaffeinated,' she reassured him.

He grimaced. 'Oh God, what's that like?'

'Exhausting,' she admitted. 'I never knew how much I needed my morning caffeine until now.'

'You're going to be fine,' Nick said supportively. 'And if you need anything, me and Amanda are always there for you.'

'Aw, thank you,' Georgie said as she turned, smiled at the woman behind the till, and used her police canteen card to pay for her coffee and toast.

For a second, Nick's mention of Amanda made her a little jealous. She knew that Nick had had his problems in the past and she was happy that he now had a stable home life with Amanda and Megan. But there was still a little bit of envy on her part too. And if she was honest, Nick was exactly the type of man she wanted to be with. Strong, caring, self-aware, funny… and good looking.

'Going back up?' he asked as he gestured over to the exit.

Georgie nodded. 'Yeah. I can't spend too much time in here. It's way too noisy.'

At this time of the morning, the canteen was full of uniformed officers having breakfast and chatting and laughing loudly.

'Yeah, I know what you mean,' Nick said with a wry smile.

They headed across the canteen, through the doors and down towards the back staircase which led up to the first floor.

'When do you have to speak to the IOPC?' Georgie asked.

'Tomorrow,' Nick said, pulling a face.

'You and Dan are telling the truth,' she said, trying to be supportive. 'So, there isn't a case to be answered.'

'Yeah, but you know what they're like,' Nick said as they walked down to the CID office. 'It's guilty until proven innocent.'

They went into the office which was relatively peaceful after the noise of the canteen and busy corridors.

As she reached her desk, Georgie sat down and took a big bite of buttery toast.

God, that's better.

Then she looked at the paperwork on her desk.

She decided to tackle it in a few minutes and logged onto her email account.

Sitting in her inbox was an email from the Colwyn Bay Medical Centre.

She clicked it open and saw that it was details she'd requested of Matty Hopkins' scooter accident.

Sitting back, she looked over the notes that detailed the extensive rehabilitation that Matty had required back in 2017.

Then she saw the date of his accident – *1 June 2017.*

That's the date that Sophie Hopkins died!

'Nick?' she called over, starting to feel uneasy about the connection she'd found.

'What's up?' he asked as he approached, his coffee still in his hand.

She gave him a quizzical look. 'The date we saw on Sophie Hopkins' grave at the church. It was the 1 June 2017, wasn't it?'

'Yes.'

She narrowed her eyes and looked up at him. 'That's the date of Matty Hopkins' scooter accident.'

Nick took a few seconds to process what she'd told him. 'Really?'

'I've been sent the medical records of his rehabilitation after the accident,' she explained as she pointed to her computer.

Nick looked over her shoulder and peered at the screen.

'That can't be a coincidence, can it?' she asked.

'I'm not sure,' Nick said, looking puzzled. 'Or was Sophie Hopkins killed in the scooter accident? Is there any way we can check that right now?'

'I can ring the records office in Colwyn Bay,' she suggested.

'I'm not sure that it's particularly relevant to our invest-igation,' Nick said, 'but I'd like to have that information.'

Garrow approached. 'Boss, digital forensics have called. They've got that CCTV from the holiday park. The stuff they sent over to Manchester.'

'Any idea if they managed to clean up the quality?'

'They didn't say,' Garrow replied. 'I can go over there now?'

Nick shook his head. 'No. I'd better go and have a look. Thanks Jim.'

CHAPTER 60

Five minutes later, Nick had crossed the road and entered the new forensics building. He approached a male digital forensics officer – twenties, short hair, dark beard and glasses.

Nick introduced himself. 'DS Evans from CID across the road.'

'Morning, sir.'

'You sent some CCTV from Pen-y-Bryn Holiday Park in Colwyn Bay over to Manchester Police to get the image cleaned up?' Nick said by way of an explanation.

'That's right,' the officer confirmed as he gestured to a nearby desk where there was a laptop. 'Actually, we now send it to a private contractor in Manchester that the MMP use. They've got the latest technology that can remove blur and pixelation. Plus, they boost the resolution. It's stuff we can't really do here.'

'Have you had a look at what they sent back yet?' Nick asked, as the officer sat down at his desk.

'Yes, about half an hour ago,' he replied as he tapped at the keyboard.

Nick sat down on a nearby chair. 'What did you think?'

'I think it's pretty good given the height of the camera and that it's at night with minimal light. Let me show you.'

After a few seconds, the CCTV appeared on the laptop monitor. As it played, the figure wearing a baseball cap appeared. The officer paused the image.

Nick moved closer and peered intently at the screen. If he was honest, he was a little disappointed by what he was looking at.

'I don't know if it's my eyesight,' Nick said, trying not to sound frustrated, 'but I can't see the person's face clearly.'

'Let's see if this works,' the officer said as he clicked on zoom.

The image zoomed in.

Nick looked again. Although the figure still wasn't clear, his instinct was that it wasn't Kevin Ball that he was looking at.

That's not good, he thought with a sinking feeling.

The officer looked over at Nick and could obviously see his disappointment.

'We could give it a go on that monitor, sir? It might be clearer,' he suggested, pointing to a large monitor that was mounted on the wall.

'Worth a try,' Nick said, but he wasn't holding out any hope.

The officer typed at the computer and the monitor on the wall flickered into life.

The CCTV footage was now up on the wall – and it had made a huge difference.

Getting up from his chair, Nick walked closer to the screen and peered at the figure who was holding two cans of petrol.

The person's face was now visible.

It was Jane Hopkins.

CHAPTER 61

Twenty minutes later, Nick was back in CID with the whole team assembled. Garrow had been sent the CCTV footage from the digital forensics officer, and it was now up on the monitor on the wall of the CID office. Everyone was gobsmacked.

'I don't get it,' French said as he peered over at the image of Jane Hopkins in a baseball cap, carrying two cans of petrol.

Nick looked at him. 'Dan, I've thought about what Kevin Ball said to us in Holyhead. He told us that he didn't want to go to prison. He said that he didn't mean to do it and that he just snapped. And he told us that Kat had slept with Matty. But he didn't reference the fire. What if he was just talking about the fact that he'd assaulted Kat that morning and thought he was going to get a custodial sentence for it?'

'Okay,' French said thoughtfully. Nick could see that he wasn't convinced.

Garrow looked over. 'If we think that Jane Hopkins was responsible for the fire and Matty's death, what's her motive?'

Georgie shifted forwards on her seat. 'We've just discovered that Jane had a daughter, Sophie, by a previous marriage. Sophie died on the 1 June 2017, which is the same date as Matty's scooter accident in which his leg was severely injured.'

Nick raised an eyebrow. 'So, do we think that she died in that accident?'

Garrow signalled that he had something important. 'Boss, I finally got an email from Colwyn Bay police station yesterday. It's the accident report from 2017. Given all that had happened with Kevin Ball, I didn't open it as a priority.'

'That's fine, Jim,' Nick reassured him. 'It wasn't a priority until now.'

'Okay,' Garrow said as he began to tap away at his computer. Then for a few seconds, he read what was on the screen before glancing up and giving Nick a dark look. 'The scooter accident happened at the holiday park at 7:25 p.m. on the 1 of June 2017. Matty Hopkins was riding the scooter. Apparently, Sophie Hopkins was a passenger on the scooter but wasn't wearing a helmet. She was pronounced dead at the scene. It happened on a private road, so the Road Traffic Act and other legislation didn't apply, and no criminal charges were brought against Matty.'

Nick nodded and looked at everyone. 'Well, now we have Jane's motive.

CHAPTER 62

Nick and French arrived at the Hopkins' house within the grounds of the holiday park with an arrest warrant for Jane. The CCTV footage was overwhelming evidence that linked her to the fire at the cabin. It seemed that whatever had happened during the scooter accident back in 2017, she must have blamed Matty for her daughter's death. And for some reason, this feeling of anger and resentment had never left her. So when the opportunity presented itself on Saturday night, Jane jumped at the opportunity to get revenge for Sophie.

Nick knocked at the door.

They waited for a few seconds but there was no answer.

French pointed to the drive where a brand-new black Range Rover Sport was parked. 'Their car is here, so they can't have gone far.'

Nick knocked again.

Nothing.

They wandered around to the back of the house where there were stables and a fenced paddock.

There was someone in the paddock with a chestnut-coloured horse.

It was Jane Hopkins.

'Jane, is it okay if we have a word?' Nick called over as they approached.

'Gosh, I've got to go and meet someone,' she said as she looked at her watch. She appeared flustered by their arrival. 'Can you come back later?'

Nick looked at French with a frown. 'Not really. We really do need to speak to you right now.'

Jane stared at them both defiantly.

There was an awkward silence.

She must have sensed that whatever they wanted to speak to her about, it was very serious.

Without warning, she put her foot in the stirrup, swung her leg over the horse, kicked her heels and galloped away.

'Are you bloody joking?' French said through gritted teeth.

Nick looked around. *What the hell do we do now?*

Then he spotted a muddy Yamaha quad bike. It gave him an idea.

Five years earlier, while very hungover, Nick had jumped on a quad bike and chased a local man, Dewi Hughes, who had escaped on a horse.

'Radio for back up,' Nick yelled as he turned and broke into a run.

'You're not going to catch her on foot,' French called out.

'I know that,' Nick shouted as he got to the quad bike and jumped on. He hit the black starter button and its engine roared into life. 'I will do on this thing though.'

He pushed down on the accelerator and sped away, past the paddock and onto the fields that seemed to stretch away into the distance.

Looking ahead, he calculated that Jane was about a hundred yards ahead of him as she galloped across the fields.

What the hell is she doing? And how the hell does she think she's going to get away?

As he took the quad bike up to 45 mph, Nick could see that he was starting to gain on Jane.

Hitting a dip, he felt the bike leave the ground for a second before crashing back down. It nearly threw him off, but he was gripping on to the handlebar grips with everything he had. The mud seemed to be flying up from under the bike and going everywhere.

With the accelerator hard to the floor, the bike was now doing 60 mph and gaining fast on the horse.

He spotted Jane glance back anxiously. There was no way she was going to get away.

Pulling the horse suddenly to the left, she galloped diagonally across the field.

Nick turned the quad bike sharply to follow and felt it go onto two wheels.

Oh God, don't let this tip over at this speed, he thought anxiously.

The bike righted itself.

Then Nick spotted why Jane had decided to change direction. In the corner of the field there was a tall, rectangular hedgerow that bordered the fields beyond. He assumed that she had calculated that if she could jump the hedge into those fields, Nick couldn't follow, and so she could make her escape.

He needed to intercept her before she got to the hedge.

Slamming down the accelerator pedal, Nick heard the twin-stroke 450cc engine roar.

Jane was only about forty yards ahead.

Her horse was throwing up great clumps of earth with its hooves.

Thirty yards.

The hedge was getting closer.

Nick ducked as another clump of earth flew past his ear.

Twenty yards.

Now that he was this close, he wasn't sure how he was going to stop her.

They were virtually at the hedgerow..

Ten yards.

Suddenly, the horse reared up as they reached the edge of the field.

Jane flew backwards and landed heavily on her back.

Hitting the brakes, Nick managed to grind the quad bike to a halt, jump off and run over.

He didn't need to worry.

Jane was winded and gasping for breath.

He looked down at her as he wiped mud from his face and hair. 'Jane Hopkins, I'm arresting you for the murder of Matty Hopkins.'

CHAPTER 63

It was late afternoon and Sarah had just arrived back at Ruth's house with a stack of takeaway pizzas for tea. While Ruth sat in the armchair in the living room with a blanket over her knees, Ella had fussed around making sure everything was neat and tidy.

Sarah came into the living room with the boxes of pizzas. 'Are we going posh and eating off plates, or common and eating out of the boxes?'

Ruth rolled her eyes. 'What do you think? Common.'

Sarah went away again and then returned. 'Someone has just got home from school and would like to say hello.'

Daniel appeared at the doorway, spotted Ruth and then sprinted across the room to give her a hug. 'Ruth!'

'Hey, easy there tiger. Remember I haven't been well,' she said, bracing herself.

Daniel took a step back. 'It's all right. I know you got shot. Hayley Peters told me at school. And then I saw it online. You're a hero, aren't you?'

'Not really,' she said. In fact, she'd been shot because she'd not been concentrating. There was nothing heroic about it at all.

'Will you get a medal?' Daniel asked excitedly. 'Maybe they'll make a film on Netflix about you?'

'Yeah, I'm not sure about any of that,' Ruth laughed.

'Who would they get to play you, Mum?' Ella asked with a grin.

'Keeley Hawes?' Ruth suggested.

'In your dreams,' Sarah snorted. 'Imelda Staunton?'

Ruth scowled and gave her the finger. 'Piss off.'

Daniel looked at Ruth. 'You swore!'

'Sorry,' Ruth said as she gave Sarah a sarcastic smile.

Sarah spread the pizza boxes around on the table, along with napkins and two huge bottles of Pepsi. 'Come on guys. Get stuck in.'

'Mum said to say hi and she'll see you tomorrow,' Sarah explained as she slumped down on the sofa next to Ella.

Daniel went and grabbed a slice of pizza and then sat at Ruth's feet. She ruffled his hair.

Ruth sighed as she looked around the room. The feeling of gratitude and love was overwhelming. 'God, it's so nice to be home.'

Ella gestured to the pizzas. 'What do you want, Mum? I'm not sure you should have the meat feast.'

'I'm fine at the moment,' Ruth said. 'In fact, while you're all here, there's something I'd like to talk to you about.'

Ella looked worried. 'That sounds ominous.'

'Not at all, darling,' Ruth reassured her. 'Obviously, being shot and being in a coma made me take stock of my life. And it made me realise what was important in my life. And that's everyone sitting in this room. And I'm kicking on a bit...'

'No you're not,' Ella protested.

'What does "kicking on" mean?' Daniel asked.

'It means I'm getting old,' Ruth laughed.

'Fifty-four isn't old,' Daniel insisted.

'Well, it's not young either,' Ruth said. 'So, I've decided that I'm going to take early retirement. I'll spend the next couple of months convalescing at home. Fill out the relevant paperwork. And that will be me done.'

'Wow,' Ella said, as her eyes widened. She got up and gave Ruth a hug. 'Good for you, Mum. I'm so pleased for you.'

CHAPTER 64

Nick leaned over and pressed the red button on the digital recording equipment. There was a long, loud electronic beep.

'Interview conducted with Jane Hopkins, Interview Room 2, Llancastell Police Station. Present are Duty Solicitor Amanda Price, Detective Sergeant Daniel French, and myself, Detective Sergeant Nick Evans.'

Jane was now dressed in a grey sweatshirt and bottoms. She looked broken and nervous.

French pulled out his pen and clicked it open. 'Jane, can you tell us where you were on Saturday night?'

Jane took a nervous gulp. 'I was at home all night.'

'Can anyone vouch for that?' he asked.

'My husband can,' she said quietly.

'You were with your husband all night?'

Jane didn't answer for a few seconds.

'Well… I think he went up to bed before me,' she said uncertainly.

'And what time do you think that was?'

'I suppose it was about eleven p.m.,' she replied.

'But you stayed in your home for the rest of the evening and then went to bed yourself. Is that correct?' French asked as he scribbled on the A4 pad in front of him.

Jane nodded. 'Yes, it is.'

Unfortunately you've just told us a huge lie.

Nick took a laptop that was already open on the table and clicked the space bar. The screen flickered and the CCTV footage from the holiday park on Saturday night appeared. He let it play until the figure appeared and then paused it.

'For the purposes of the tape, I'm showing the suspect Item Reference 397H,' he said as he turned the screen for Jane to look at. 'Could you tell us what you can see on the screen, Jane?'

She leaned forwards and peered at the screen. The blood drained from her face when she saw what was on the footage.

There were a few seconds of awkward silence.

Jane, who was now visibly shaking, leaned into Price and they whispered in low voices for a second.

She cast her eyes to Nick and French. 'No comment,' she said, her voice trembling.

Oh great, Nick thought in frustration.

'Okay, I'm going to tell you what we can see in this footage,' Nick said. 'It clearly shows you with two cans of petrol in your hands in Pen-y-Bryn Holiday Park at 11:45 p.m. Could you explain why you were carrying two petrol cans through the park at that time when you've just told us that you were at home?'

She shifted awkwardly in her seat. 'No comment.'

'Fifteen minutes after this footage was recorded, someone poured petrol onto Cabin 5 and set it alight. Is there anything you can tell us about that, Jane?'

Jane's leg was jigging uncontrollably. 'No comment,' she whispered.

French studied her carefully before speaking. 'Did you deliberately set fire to that cabin?'

She pursed her lips and shook her head. 'No comment.'

'Unfortunately, your stepson, Matty, had let himself into that vacant cabin to sleep off a heavy night's drinking,' French said. 'Did you see him going into the cabin?'

Jane was now staring at the floor. She shook her head. It seemed like she was completely overwhelmed.

Nick reached out, took a folder and pulled out a document. 'For the purposes of the tape, I'm showing the suspect Item Reference 328J. This is a police report of an accident that occurred at the holiday park on 1 June 2017.' Nick tried to lock eyes with Jane but she was shaking and looking down at the floor. 'Does that date mean anything to you, Jane?'

'No comment,' she whispered so that it was barely audible.

'According to the police report, your stepson Matty was driving a scooter on a private road in the grounds of the park that evening. Your daughter, who was six years old at the time, was riding on the back of the scooter...' Nick paused for a moment before continuing, '...and she was killed. Is that correct?'

Jane began to sob. It was all too much for her.

Nick waited for a few seconds. 'Jane,' he said gently. 'I really need you to tell us what happened on Saturday night.'

'I can't,' she wept. 'I can't do that.'

'Jane, we just need you to tell us the truth,' he said softly, 'because it's going to come out anyway. So this is your chance to tell us what happened.'

Price handed Jane a tissue and she dabbed the tears from her eyes. She took a long deep breath and looked across at them. 'Saturday was Sophie's birthday,' she said shakily. 'She would have been ten years old.'

Nick gave her an empathetic nod. 'It must have been a difficult day for you.'

'It was,' Jane said as her eyes filled with tears again. 'It always is. And Matty has never really taken responsibility for what happened. I know it was an accident, but it was his idea for Sophie to go out with him.'

'I guess you must have had a lot of anger towards Matty since the accident?' Nick suggested.

Jane nodded as she took another deep breath and tried to compose herself. 'I've tried not to. But he seems to have no guilt about what happened whatsoever.' She caught herself using the present tense. 'He didn't... I do honestly think that he was a sociopath. He didn't seem to have any empathy for anyone. And he treated everyone that was close to him so badly. Some of the things he'd say to Miles were horrendous.'

She then reached for a glass of water. Her hand shook as she tried to take a sip.

'I told Matty on Saturday afternoon that it would have been Sophie's tenth birthday,' Jane explained as she put the glass down. 'And he just gave me this look. This horrible look of utter contempt. Then he shrugged as if it didn't mean anything to him and said 'Okay'. And then he gave this little laugh as if he had no idea why I'd told him. And then he walked off with a smirk.' Jane shook her head. 'I was so angry. So, so angry.'

'Can you tell us what happened on Saturday night?' Nick asked.

'Miles went to bed. I took the dogs out for a walk,' Jane said. 'And then I saw him...'

'Matty?' French asked to clarify.

'Yes. He was completely hammered and could hardly walk. I didn't say anything. I was still so angry with him.

And I watched as he let himself into the cabin. After a few minutes, I went over. I opened the door and saw that he was lying on the sofa completely out of it. So, I locked him in.'

'Why did you lock him in the cabin?' French asked.

'You know what, I have no idea,' she admitted. 'I took the dogs back home. And then, in a moment of utter madness, I took those petrol cans, went over to the cabin and set it on fire. And I watched it burn.'

There was a long silence.

Nick looked over at French and then at Jane. 'Jane Hopkins, I'm charging you with the murder of Matty Hopkins.'

CHAPTER 65

JULY 2021

Three months later

It was nine a.m. as Ruth entered Llancastell nick. It felt so incredibly surreal. So familiar, but also as if she hadn't been there for years. As she made her way through the ground floor, there was a series of smiles and waves from uniformed officers.

Sergeant Brooker, who was sitting at reception, looked over and gave her a toothy grin. 'Good to see you back safe and sound, ma'am.'

'Good to be back,' Ruth said as she headed for the back staircase that led to the first floor and the CID office.

There were more smiles as she made her way down the corridor. She arrived at the double doors marked CID and took a moment. She had no idea how the CID team were going to react to what she was going to tell them. She had been backwards and forwards with her decision a hundred times in the past three months.

Taking a deep breath, she pushed open the doors.

For a moment, the office was almost silent.

Detectives were working at desks and typing at computers.

Well I wasn't looking for a rousing fanfare, but some acknow-ledgement that I'm back would be nice, she thought, trying not to be indignant.

Nick and Georgie appeared from around the corner, grinning. They were holding a banner that read – *SHE'S BACK! THANK GOD! xx*

The whole office erupted into laughter, clapping and cheering.

'Oh very bloody funny,' Ruth said, shaking her head with a beaming smile.

Nick and Georgie came over and gave her a hug.

Ruth then looked out at the assembled CID team and felt a little overwhelmed by their smiling faces and cheers.

She held up her hands and laughed. 'Yeah, all right, you lot. Settle down.'

'Great to have you back, boss,' French called over.

Ruth hesitated as they began to quieten. 'Listen, I just have a few words to say and then I'll shut up and you can get on with your work.' She took a deep breath. 'Being shot, having a cardiac arrest and nearly dying has definitely changed the way I look at life now. And I've had three months at home, and I've done a lot of thinking. I've thought about what's important in my life. My family and friends.' Ruth perched herself on a nearby table. She could see that some of the CID team were now concerned about what she was going to tell them. 'And you all know how much this job, being a police officer, has meant to me over the years. And moving to North Wales and getting to know you all has been such a wonderful experience.' She looked over at Nick and Georgie. 'And I've heard there have been rumours that I'm going to take early retirement, and I felt you should hear it from me first.'

For a moment, the whole office went silent.

Ruth grinned. 'You're not going to get rid of me that easily, you buggers.'

There was more cheering and a huge sense of relief.

A phone rang on a desk at the back of the office and Garrow answered in a hushed voice.

'Being at home for three months nearly drove me insane,' Ruth admitted. 'My daughter Ella is at work all day. Daniel is at school. And Sarah is spending a lot of her time caring for her mother. So, I was actually on my own and very bored. So you're stuck with me for a bit longer, I'm afraid.'

'That's great news,' Georgie said as she came over.

Nick approached and said under his breath, 'I knew it.'

Ruth looked to the back of the office where Garrow had put down the phone. 'Everything all right, Jim?' she asked.

'Not really, boss,' he replied.

'What's up?'

'Uniformed officers have found a body in Oswestry,' he explained.

Ruth frowned. 'Oswestry is in England, isn't it?'

'Yes, boss. But they believe the victim is Welsh and that he was murdered somewhere in North Wales,' Garrow said.

'Right,' Ruth said thoughtfully. Then she turned to Nick and threw him her car keys.

'Where are we going?' he asked uncertainly.

'I can't sit here chatting all day,' she replied with a knowing smile. 'We're going to England and we've got a murder to solve. You drive, I'll smoke.'

'I thought you quit?'

'Come on,' Ruth groaned as she headed for the double doors.

Your FREE book is waiting for you NOW

THE THEATRE STREET KILLING PREQUEL

South London 1995. A brutal murder.

Find out about Ruth Hunter and her move from Uniform to being a detective in CID.

Get your free prequel at

http://www.simonmccleave.com/vip-email-club

and join my VIP Email Club.

canelo
CRIME

Do you love crime fiction and are always on the lookout for brilliant authors?

Canelo Crime is home to some of the most exciting novels around. Thousands of readers are already enjoying our compulsive stories. Are you ready to find your new favourite writer?

Find out more and sign up to our newsletter at canelocrime.com